The Winning Bid

The Auction Series

Book One

Michelle Windsor

First Published in October 2016
Copyright © Michelle Windsor 2016

Published by
Windsor House Publishing

Cover Design by Jessica Hildreth at Creative Book Concepts

Editing by Elizabeth Nover at Razor Sharp Editing

For my mom, who always believed I could do this, and for Doug, who let me.

Chapter One

Naked and nervous, Hannah wondered if she was making the right decision. She knew what to expect but still shivered as she stood in line waiting for the auction to begin. It was too late to turn back now. The auction would begin in moments. There were six other women and two men standing with her, but unlike her, they were flushed and heated with anticipation. Two of the girls were practically panting.

Domme Maria, owner of Baton Timide, strutted down the line, loudly clapping her hands and drawing the attention of each submissive. "All right, my little slaves, submission begins now!"

She opened the door and held it wide as each submissive stepped through onto the adjoining stage, assuming their submissive position as trained. Hannah's heart hammered in her chest as each second brought her closer to her turn. Standing in the doorway twenty seconds later, Domme Maria hustled her onstage with a slap on the ass.

She darted across the stage and knelt in the customary submissive position: hands open flat on her spread thighs, head and eyes down. The heat of the spotlight instantly warmed her nude body. She had never been on such blatant display before and was surprised at the surge of excitement that ran through her. Murmurs and exclamations of appreciation from the crowd rolled through her like thunder before a storm. She desperately wanted to lift her head and see the people in the room. It was her first time attending an auction and was curious to see if the room was filled with men, or if women were present too. And would the men be handsome, or older and more lecherous. Unable to resist, she tilted her head up just a pinch and peeked through her eyelashes to try and capture a brief glimpse of the crowd. Her eyes immediately locked on a dark-haired gentleman staring right at her. Her face heated in embarrassment, and she quickly lowered her head and eyes, praying that no one else had noticed.

Only Master-level Dominant members of the exclusive club, Baton Timide, were allowed to participate in submissive auctions. They had to be a VIP member as well, which basically just meant they had to be filthy rich. She was a new submissive—a fact she hoped would push her bidding price higher. Dominants loved to break in new submissives and would pay dearly for the privilege.

Auctioned submissives made twenty-five percent of the winning bid. The house took seventy-five percent. The minimum starting bid was fifteen thousand dollars, so she figured she could, at the very least, walk away with almost four thousand dollars for a few days' work—four thousand dollars closer to her dream, her own shop. The owner of the shop she worked in was retiring and had agreed to sell it to her at an amazing price. The only caveat: the thirty-thousand-dollar down payment to secure the loan was due in three months. With no savings, no rich family and no fairy godmother waiting in the wings, this auction was her only hope.

Behind Hannah, Domme Maria closed the door the girls had just come through, and her black leather boots came to a stop at the center of the stage. She was quite an intimidating force, with dark hair that gleamed like silk, a face that was almost porcelain white, and lips always painted a blood red to accent her crisp blue eyes. Hannah could only guess how the club members perceived the Domme, but after training with her, the stunning woman could bring Hannah to her knees with a single glance.

"Welcome, ladies and gentlemen. It is my great pleasure, and hopefully yours, to bring you nine submissives to choose from this evening."

Domme Marie smiled, turned and waved her hand toward the line of kneeling submissives. Then she strolled to the first person in the row. She stroked the girl's long, flaxen hair like she was a new pet and ordered the sub to stand. Like Vanna White displaying a new puzzle, she presented the girl with a flourish. "Let me present Lahna, one of our more experienced submissives. She has no hard limits and quite thoroughly enjoys a bit of pain."

At that statement, Domme Maria took the black leather riding crop in her hand and smacked Lahna across her breasts, leaving a bright red welt. In turn, Lahna's head fell back as she moaned not in pain, but in distinct pleasure. Hannah was shocked by the sight. She'd expected to be showcased, but not to be so blatantly excited by it. And Lahna wasn't the only one affected. Peeking under her lashes and out across the people in the room again, Hannah saw one gentleman adjust himself as he moved closer to the display area.

While Domme Maria continued the introductions, Hannah discreetly continued her investigation of the room, her attention falling on the gentleman she'd locked eyes with earlier. As her gaze moved upward, she realized he was staring right back at her again. Instead of hiding her head this time, she lifted it just a fraction and boldly met his eye. He was breathtakingly handsome. His dark hair was smoothed back from his face but long enough to hit the collar on the black suit jacket he wore. A thin coating of stubble lent him a rough look, but it was his eyes that mesmerized her. They were dark, almond shaped and framed with a set of dark, full eyelashes. He was too far away for Hannah to be sure what color they were. As she continued to stare, the corner of his eyes crinkled as if he was stifling a laugh, and a slow grin spread across his face. Hannah broke eye contact and looked down again quickly. His grin was that of a feral hunter, and she just might be his prey.

Domme Maria continued down the row of submissives, displaying and touting each one's specialties and hard limits, until suddenly she was behind Hannah. The Domme lovingly stroked Hannah's long, wavy hair but then suddenly grasped it firmly and yanked her head back. Hannah's chest thrust forward, and a small yelp of surprise escaped her.

"This very lovely lady is Scarlett, and this is her first time at one of our auctions." Domme Maria looked down, then kissed Hannah lightly on the lips before releasing her hair and gesturing for her to stand up.

As she stood, Domme Maria surveyed the bidders and, with a sly smile, continued, "And oh yes, she does taste as delicious as she looks. She is a bit like a scared kitten though, with many hard limits, and will require a Master with patience to show her the pleasure in breaking some of those limits." She stopped and scanned the room again before continuing, "And believe me, as I have personally trained her, there is a tigress waiting to emerge." Domme Maria skimmed her hand down Hannah's—no, *Scarlett's* body, stopping to cup her firm breast and pinch her nipple sharply, and then walked on to the next submissive.

Hannah dropped immediately into the submissive position again, looking down and taking a deep breath to try and calm her pounding heart. She was shocked to realize her heart beat with excitement, not fear. And shock at the warm feeling between her legs when Domme Maria had pinched her nipple. *This is definitely something I can do.* She could perform this role. Here, she was Scarlett, not Hannah. She could be whomever she chose to be, without any shame. Any doubts and fears she'd had evaporated, and excitement began to course through her instead.

Hannah knew she had made the correct choice for an alternate identity. When asked what name she'd wanted to be called, she had chosen Scarlett. Hannah was a closet romantic, and even though she had no illusions about finding Rhett and living happily ever after, she loved what the name stood for. Scarlett O'Hara had been fearless, breaking boundaries for the things she loved and believed in. Hannah was here for the same reasons.

Domme Maria finished introducing the last submissive for auction and retook center stage. "Ladies and gentleman, at this time, if you would like to personally inspect any of the submissives for auction, please do so, but keep in mind the rules of engagement prior to purchase. You may look, speak and touch—with the permission of the submissive only—but nothing more. You have exactly one hour before bidding begins." With that, Domme Maria strode off the stage and down to greet the bidders in the room.

There were only a dozen bidders at the auction, so the inspection period really didn't require a great length of time. But an hour of anticipation, on your knees, in submissive form, could seem like ten. Hannah kept her head down, trying to busy her mind and remain still and patient.

Drew took a sip of his gin martini and casually appraised each submissive walking through the door. He was happy to see Jenna take a place onstage. He'd purchased the submissive at two previous auctions and had hoped she would be present again. The last three weeks had been hell, and he really needed this weekend to relieve some much needed stress, and without any of the practicalities that a new submissive always required.

Having already made up his mind about his bid this evening, he was about to turn away and take a seat in the back of the room when the next woman walked out onto the stage. Her head was down, her long, straw-colored hair hiding her features, yet he knew he'd never seen her before at an auction, or at any of the club events. He would have remembered.

Even without seeing her face, he knew she would be beautiful. She was petite. Not skin and bones, but perfect curves of honey-colored skin. Her breasts—tipped with small, dark pink nipples, already peaked and ready—would fit nicely into his hands. *Or better yet*, he thought, *in my mouth*. Her hips flared only slightly, but they weren't boyish, as her ass arched with a soft, yielding roundness.

As she stopped on the stage and knelt, she peeked up quickly, and in that instant, her eyes caught his. She immediately looked down again, cheeks flushing, palms flat on her spread thighs. Her hands trembled slightly, and he realized then that she must be a new submissive. He also realized his plans to purchase Jenna for the weekend had just gone out the window, practicalities be damned.

He paid particular attention as Domme Maria introduced the unknown blonde. *Her name is Scarlett.* And seeing her face now, albeit from a distance, he could see that she was in fact beautiful. She gasped in surprise when Maria pulled her head back, but then softened when the Domme's lips met hers in a gentle kiss. When Maria tweaked Scarlett's nipple, her nervous energy disappeared. Her breath quickened and her body flushed a light pink, revealing her excitement. She may be a new submissive, but her behavior indicated she was made to be dominated. He had to have her.

He listened as Domme Maria finished the introductions and offered the submissives up for inspection. From the back of the room, Drew remained in his chair, still sipping his gin, and waited to see what happened. He needed to appear almost aloof so as not to pique the interest or the challenging nature of some of the other Dominants in this room. In particular, he watched one of the other club members, Deacon Roberts. He was well known for his preference for new submissives. There was no doubt that Roberts would throw his hat in the ring for a chance at Scarlett.

Just as expected, within ten minutes of the introductions being completed, Roberts made his way to the stage and stopped directly in front of Scarlett. Drew got up and casually strolled closer, where refreshments were being served, and pretended to be interested in the appetizers so he could listen to the exchange between Benson and the new submissive.

Hannah's neck was starting to feel a bit sore from keeping her head down. She was tempted to reach up and rub the back of it, but of course knew better. She remained still and waited patiently for whatever happened next, as trained. A pair of brown wing-tip shoes stopped in front of her, their owner looming over her. She wondered if it was the man she had locked eyes with. Or hoped, to tell the truth.

If she was going to spend a weekend at someone's beck and call, why shouldn't that someone look mighty fine as well? A strong voice interrupted her thoughts and snapped her back to attention.

"Please rise, Scarlett. I'd like to inspect you." Hannah drew up from her knees, standing straight but continuing to look down, as taught. This wasn't her mystery man after all. *He* had worn a black suit, while this gentleman's suit was a darker tan. The man's breath ghosted over her skin, he was so close, and she caught a faint trace of whiskey on his breath. He finally spoke, ordering her to raise her head and look straight ahead. She did as she was told and was finally able to get a better look at him from her peripheral vision. He was five or six inches taller than she was and had dark blonde hair with darker blue eyes. About thirty-five or forty, he seemed to have a fairly good build. She stifled a sigh of relief. At least he wasn't hideous.

"Scarlett, may I touch you?" As had been explained to her in training, bidders were encouraged to check potential purchases for firmness of breast, or state of grooming, or smoothness of skin. She knew to consent immediately or risk not being bid on.

"Yes, Sir."

He nodded, then added under his breath, "Well, aren't you a good little submissive. So eager. So ready to please." He stroked a finger down the side of her neck and then back up toward her mouth. Hooking his finger into her mouth, he pulled it open harshly. "Oh yes, I think this mouth would fit quite well around my cock."

Hannah's eyes widened in surprise, and she had to force herself not to retreat as the man stepped closer. He trailed his finger down to the juncture between her legs, then prodded her clit before pushing in just a little bit. "And this? I think I'll enjoy putting my cock in here even more."

Hannah tensed as the man spoke even more softly into her ear, "Oh yes, breaking you will be so much fun," and turned and walked off the stage. She stood, shocked, still staring ahead, as he barked one more order. "Kneel, Scarlett!" And she did, complying immediately.

Drew couldn't hear the exchange between Roberts and the new submissive, but he saw the fear in her eyes, as well as her body go rigid at his touch, and knew that Roberts had most likely crossed a line. Inside, rage soared, a possessiveness and a need to protect this girl overtaking him. It was a feeling he hadn't experienced before. But no matter its origin, he had to stay his course and remain calm so Roberts wouldn't notice his interest in Scarlett.

Drew decided not to go up and investigate her for fear of triggering Roberts' competitive nature. But he did want to get a closer look at this new submissive. So instead, he walked up on the stage, stopped in front of Jenna and asked her to rise. Jenna's posture straightened in obvious happiness, and he was hit with a moment of regret, knowing she would be disappointed when he did not bid on her.

"Jenna, you may look at me." Jenna lifted her head and smiled. She really was quite lovely. She was taller than average and possessed the body and grace of a dancer. Her short pixie cut suited her dark hair and exotic, angled features.

"How have you been, Jenna? You look lovely as always."

Her eyes sparkled with desire, and she responded breathily, "I am very well, Master. It is very nice to see you again. Have you been well, Sir?"

Drew looked down, shook his head and smiled. "Now Jenna, are you supposed to ask a Master a question?"

Jenna cast her eyes downward. "I'm sorry, Master. I meant no disrespect."

Drew couldn't help but notice Scarlett's head tilt slightly in their direction. A surge of satisfaction ran through him at the realization that she was listening to his conversation with Jenna. Just as quickly, another wave of guilt washed over him. No doubt Jenna would feel betrayed after his current attention didn't lead to a weekend together.

Drew smiled warmly and almost apologetically before taking Jenna's hand, kissing her knuckles kindly. "Kneel, Jenna, and be well."

Jenna kneeled immediately as he turned and walked back the way he'd come. He stopped, just for a moment, to look down at Scarlett. His hand rose to stroke her hair, but he stopped himself, drawing it quickly back to his side before continuing down off the stage.

Domme Maria made an announcement shortly thereafter: bidding for the submissives was now open. Each Dominant could submit a starting bid for any given submissive. Once all bids were submitted, if a submissive garnered only one bid, Maria would text that bidder to let them know they'd won. If multiple bidders bid on a single submissive, Maria would text them all a request for a higher bid. No one would know who bid on which submissive. Each bidder was allowed a maximum of three bids on any one submissive. The highest bid after three rounds won.

Drew waited until every other Dominant had met with Maria before approaching her.

She smiled sweetly, if not seductively. "Master Drew, it is always a pleasure when you are in my house. Can I hope that you'll be placing a bid tonight?"

Drew took Maria's hand, swept his lips across her knuckles and graced her with one of his most charming smiles. She always felt so cold to him. "The pleasure is all mine, Madame. And yes, I will be placing a bid this evening."

He presented her a slip of paper with his bid for Scarlett: $25,000. Maria took the ticket and then nodded at him with a raised eyebrow.

"Well, this is a bit of a surprise. Not your usual taste." A small smile curved her lips. "This should make for a very interesting night. Your girl has two other bids. Good luck."

"Thank you, Madame. May the best man win, right?"

Drew turned but not before Maria added one final word. "You mean may the best *Dom* win."

Drew went to the bar and asked for another gin martini. He usually had only one drink at these affairs, but to his surprise, he found himself a bit anxious, knowing Scarlett had two other bidders. Certainly Roberts was one of the bidders, but who could the other be? No one else had approached or inspected her. He slowly swept his eyes across the room to see if anyone's body language gave them away. He stopped on Roberts, who looked up at him and nodded. Drew nodded back and continued his search of the room. His phone buzzed with a text message: "High bid is currently $25K. Please submit new bid if so desired."

Well, at least he was the highest bidder so far. Now was the tricky part, what to bid next? As rich as Drew, Roberts was the only other Dom in the room who could compete. And like Drew, Roberts usually went after what he wanted, damn the cost. Drew decided to bid conservatively and submitted $30K.

Several minutes went by, and his phone buzzed with another text message: "High bid is currently $30.5K. Please submit a new bid if so desired." Drew scratched at the stubble on his chin and looked around the room. His gaze stopped on Maria, who was smiling broadly. She loved a good duel if nothing else. She nodded at him, just slightly, so as not to bring attention to herself from the other Dom's bidding. The other bidders were bidding conservatively. Time to take the opposite strategy and go large. He wanted this submissive, and he was going to make sure the other bidders knew it. It was the final bid, and he did not want to lose. He sent a text back with $50K. And waited.

After what seemed like an eternity but was really only four minutes, Drew's phone buzzed with another text: "Congratulations. You have won the bid. Your submissive will be delivered to your bungalow in thirty minutes. Please provide payment before your departure." Drew heaved a sigh of relief, then felt a surge of victory as he sat back and finished his martini.

Chapter Two

After the bidding began, each submissive was escorted from the stage and into a comfortable sitting area. Each sub was provided a robe and a glass of water. Hannah practically gulped hers down. Between her nerves and being on display like an animal at the zoo, she was desperately parched. One of Maria's attendants, Lexie, came into the room and took a seat with everyone.

"For our more experienced submissives, you know what happens next." Lexie looked at Lahna, Jenna and the other experienced subs and nodded. "But for the new submissives, Scarlett and Helena, let me just review what will happen next."

Lexie switched her focus to Hannah and Helena and continued, "In about fifteen minutes, one of the attendants will bring you to the residence you will be occupying this weekend. When you arrive, you are to go into the living room. Remove your robe, and then kneel in the submissive position until your Master arrives."

Hannah's heart pounded in anticipation, finally grasping how real the decision she'd made to sell herself had just become.

"Now, this is the hard part—the waiting, the not knowing who your Master will be for the weekend. Please try not to be too nervous. Remember everything you've learned in your training sessions. Your Master should ask you for a safe word almost immediately. Don't be afraid to use it if you need to, but also remember, once the safe word is used, the weekend is over, and the amount of money you make will be prorated for the amount of time your services were actually provided."

Would the man that had so *intimately* inspected her be her Master? Because she would quite possibly need to use a safe word if so. While all of the Doms had been provided their submissives' soft and hard limits, she had to wonder just how far she would be willing to go to earn the money she needed. There was something about the blonde that just screamed a need for control, and she was afraid he might use a lot of pain to get it.

Lexie stopped again, looked at everyone and said, "You have one job: be submissive. From 8:00 p.m. this evening until 5:00 p.m. Sunday evening. Any questions?"

Surprisingly, Lahna, who had scared Hannah a bit after the demonstration onstage, leaned forward and took her hand. "Don't worry, Scarlett. You'll be fine. Just remember what you learned, don't question your Master, and you may even enjoy yourself." She squeezed Hannah's hand before letting go.

"Thank you." Hannah was truly touched. Finding any kind of solidarity was not anything she'd expected within a group of submissives. "I really appreciate hearing that. I have to admit, I'm more nervous than I thought I would be."

Lexie rose then, and at the same time, nine attendants arrived to take each sub to their weekend residences.

Hannah's attendant introduced herself as Rose. Wearing an angelic white dress, she was extremely soft-spoken and only seemed to speak when absolutely necessary. She had shoulder-length, strawberry-blonde hair and the softest, palest complexion Hannah had ever seen. She led Hannah to a golf cart and started off on one of the paths to the many private residences nestled throughout Baton Timide's property.

The sky was starting to darken earlier now, a reminder that summer was ending and fall was beginning. Only an hour outside of New York City, the estate was like another world, given the dense forest that surrounded them. Between the night air and the very light robe Hannah was wearing, she started to shiver.

"I'm sorry. Are you cold Scarlett?" Rose questioned quietly from her side of the cart.

Hannah nodded her head to indicate she was, "A little bit."

"We won't be but another moment." Rose looked over at her with an apologetic look on her face, "We haven't brought the heavier robes out yet. I'll remind Domme Maria that it may be time."

"Thank you Rose."

As promised, Rose pulled up in front of a bungalow within a matter of minutes. She led Hannah to the front door and opened it. "You are aware of your next instruction?" Rose asked quietly.

"Yes, I am to disrobe and wait in my submissive pose until my Master arrives."

"Very good. I will take my leave now. Have a good evening." And with that, Rose walked out of the bungalow and shut the door quietly behind her.

Hannah wanted to explore the bungalow, even though she had been given a tour of one previously. It was different, knowing this is where she would stay all weekend. Where she would experience . . . well, she wasn't sure what she would experience. Time would answer that question. But she knew she had to comply with the directions given or face punishment. Domme Maria had advised all the submissives that there were cameras throughout the house to monitor behavior. Hannah was quite sure taking a tour would not fall into the good behavior department.

As instructed, she went into the bedroom and left her robe on a hook in the dressing room. There were hangers upon hangers of different outfits: dresses, suits, costumes. She so wanted to run her fingers through them but turned away, shut the door and went into the living room. She positioned herself beside the couch, faced the door and kneeled as required.

As Hannah waited, her thoughts turned again to the identity of her new Master. Even if the scary blonde was her Master, she was there to do whatever made her Dom happy, which should thus result in him treating her well. She had no doubt that she could perform sexually. She liked sex and was actually looking forward to being more submissive. Her everyday life was so regimented and required so much control all of the time. It would be nice to not have to think and just let someone else be in charge. But the few sexual partners she'd had in the past had always involved a relationship. Not knowing who she would be with, or what this person would be like, was a bit frightening. Some Dominants thrived on punishment and humiliation. She silently prayed for a kind Dominant while reminding herself that this weekend was the only solution to obtaining the money she needed without actually selling herself on a street corner. Hopefully this sacrifice could provide the security she needed.

Hannah was beginning to wonder if her Master was ever going to arrive. She had been down on her knees for at least forty-five minutes and was beginning to lose the feeling in her legs. Plus, she was cold. She hadn't had enough time to warm up in the bungalow before having to strip naked again. She was also starting to get hungry, her stomach letting out a small growl at the thought of food. And thirsty too, now that she was thinking about it. Listening to the clock tick, she tried to keep her thoughts focused on keeping her position.

Footsteps on the porch caused her heart to race, erasing all other concerns from her mind. She made sure her legs were spread apart appropriately, then placed her hands palm up on her thighs and let her gaze slip to the floor. *Please, god, let this work out okay.* The door clicked open and then shut again quietly. She wanted to look up so badly to see who her Master would be, but she dared not break a rule so soon.

Instead of footsteps coming into the living room, she heard a jacket being removed and placed on what sounded like a chair. It was amazing what your brain could decipher by sound alone when required. Then the footsteps headed toward the kitchen. The refrigerator was opened, and something was removed. Then a glass was taken down from a cupboard, and a drawer was rifled through. A pop, and then liquid was poured not once, but twice. Then footsteps again, but this time walking toward her. They stopped in front of her, and two glasses were set down on a table before he moved and sat on the couch closest to her. It was then that she noticed the shoes in front of her weren't brown. They were black— and definitely not wing tips. She almost sighed in relief, but . . .

Who did *buy me, then?*

Drew took his time arriving at the bungalow. He had finished his drink at the clubhouse and then decided to walk to the residence. He'd wanted time to think about the direction he was going to take with this submissive. It was clear from the auction display that she was new, and she was also nervous. But when she'd met his stare and hadn't backed down, he'd also known there was a strength in her that would need a little bit of bending and molding. More than anything, he really wanted to *look* at her.

The short eye contact they'd had wasn't enough for him to really assess her. He'd hated not going up and speaking with her at the auction, but his strategy had worked. He was quite sure that if Roberts had known who his opponent was, Drew would have ended up paying sixty thousand instead of fifty. Not that the money mattered. He made that much in interest every hour. One of the perks to being a billionaire that he didn't mind enjoying.

He walked quickly up the steps of the bungalow and entered. She was waiting for him, kneeling submissively, in the living room. Just seeing her like that, and knowing it was for him, instantly fueled his lust. Instead of going to her, he removed his jacket and then walked to the kitchen to retrieve a bottle of water. She had been waiting for some time and was probably thirsty, if not hungry. If he was being truly honest with himself, he also needed a moment to gather his frayed control before speaking with her.

He took two glasses from the cupboard, filled each with the water he had opened and then made his way back into the living room. He placed the glasses down on a side table, stopping to gaze down at her a moment before sitting down on the couch. Much to Drew's enjoyment, she never broke her submissive position. She evidently already wanted to please him and she didn't even know who he was yet. He leaned forward to caress the long, wavy tresses away from Scarlett's face, pushing them over her shoulders and down her back. She shivered, and he wanted to do what he could to make her feel safe and unafraid.

"Scarlett, rise and stand before me, please." Drew spoke softly so as not to scare her.

She rose immediately and stood before him, blonde hair cascading almost to her lower back, some falling forward to conceal her breasts. And he had been correct—her face was as beautiful as her body. She had a heart-shaped face with a bit of a long chin that was balanced by her lips, a soft pink and full. A petite nose—not quite a button, but it could only be described as cute, small, straight. But it was her eyes that captivated him. They were the color of caramel, the lightest shade of brown, almost golden. They were surrounded by thick lashes, unusual for a fair-haired woman. He guessed her to be twenty-four, possibly twenty-five. He stood and placed a finger under her chin, tilting her face upward so he could see her eyes more closely. They had chocolate flecks in them. In the right light, he was sure those flecks shimmered.

She said nothing but kept her eyes glued to his, and he admired her for it. She would be a good sub. He remained silent and swept her hair back over her shoulders. He backed up and looked at her now, really looked at her. Onstage, she'd been beautiful; up close, she was a knockout. Her breasts really were perfection. He loved the small nipples peaking under his examination. He wanted to touch her, but not yet. He wanted her to feel comfortable first, and she was shaking with nerves.

He cupped her face, again tilting it to him, and said, "You don't need to be afraid of me, Scarlett. I will not hurt you. I hope to bring you more joy and fulfillment over this weekend than you have ever had with a man before."

"Sir, I'm not afraid of you. I'm cold," Hannah murmured. It was the first time he had heard her voice, and it was like the most beautiful notes of music were being played. Stifling his reaction to that melody, he responded to her needs instead.

"I apologize. Please tell me immediately if you are ever uncomfortable." Drew turned, walked into the bedroom and came out with a fur blanket that had been on the end of the bed. He wrapped it around her, then motioned toward the couch. "Please, sit down."

Hannah sat and pulled the blanket closer around herself. The fur was luxuriously soft against her skin, and she was already beginning to warm. She was still in a bit of shock from discovering the very man she had made eye contact with at the auction had purchased her. She watched as he moved to the thermostat on the wall to turn up the heat. "Thank you, Master."

He turned and smiled pleasantly at her while returning to the couch, sitting next to her.

"You may call me Drew or you may address me as Sir. I only request that you reply appropriately when addressed." He shifted and reached for one of the water glasses he had brought into the room, then handed it to her. "It's seltzer water with lime. Very light and refreshing."

"Thank you, Sir." She took the glass from him and sipped it. It was delicious, and anything in her stomach right now felt wonderful.

He brought the second glass to his lips. She watched as the liquid met his mouth, how his lips arched around the rim of the glass. The short stubble outlining his chin and mouth was in stark contrast to the elegance of the glass he held. As he sipped, he looked over the glass at her, his eyes intense. She could see now that his eyes were actually a very dark blue. Was he Irish? No, then they would have been green. Perhaps Greek? When his dark brows furrowed in thought, it gave him an edge, a gravity beyond his years. He was, what, thirty-five? He pulled his glass away from his mouth and placed it on the table.

"Let's start with some preliminaries. We must pick a safe word, although I hope you never have to use it. My goal as your Master is to make you feel safe and bring you contentment, which in turn will make me happy."

Hannah nodded. "Yes, Sir. Do you have a word you would like me to use?"

Drew shook his head. "We can use the standard 'yellow' if you are at a point where I make you nervous, but you must choose the actual word. Choose a word that you won't use in everyday conversation but one that will be at the tip of your tongue if needed."

Without any further thought, Hannah blurted out, "Ghost."

Drew nodded in acceptance. "If you ever feel unsafe or scared or like you're going to break, use this word. But only in those instances. In normal circumstances, we would have more time and I would learn what your boundaries are, but in the course of three days, this obviously isn't possible."

Hannah nodded and sipped more of her water. Between the blanket and the heat blowing through the vents, she was beginning to feel quite warm again.

"Domme Maria gave me the list of your hard limits. I have no issue with any of them and understand the need for most of them. I would like to discuss the option of possibly altering one or two of them though, once you have gained more trust in me. Is that something you are open to?"

"Which limits would you like to change, Sir?"

Drew reached for his water and took a sip before responding. "Well, I'd like you to reconsider swallowing."

Hannah blushed and, taking a large gulp, finished off the rest of the water in her glass.

Drew chuckled at her reaction and then continued, "I'm sorry. I know this is an awkward discussion to have, but much better to have it now than later. When we are in the act and your warm mouth is sucking my cock, I will not want to stop. I will want to enjoy that moment. Do you understand?"

Hannah blushed crimson at his bluntness, a bit mortified at having to actually discuss her aversion to giving a blow job. "Yes, Sir, I understand. I would like to give you this pleasure, but I'm afraid I'll throw it back up on you. It's just never been my thing. I'm sorry."

Drew laughed. "All right, well, let's chalk that up to a maybe. Perhaps I can get you to change your mind. I also want to define what entails excessive pain methods for you."

Hannah nodded again, now going a bit pale as she wondered how far over her own personal boundaries she may actually have to go. In training, it had seemed so easy to safe word out. But in the here and now . . . "Okay. What do you want to know?"

Drew rose off the couch, took Hannah's glass and started walking into the kitchen. "Let me get you another glass of water, and we can finish discussing." Drew was back within a moment and handed her a refilled glass before settling back down on the couch.

"Okay, pain. Can I use clamps? Nipples and on your clit?"

Hannah nodded in response, gulping almost audibly. "Yes, as long as they aren't weighted or too tight."

"Okay, very good. What about cuffs? I know you agreed to be

restrained, but are you opposed to metal, zip ties, ropes?"

Hannah couldn't believe she was discussing this, even though Domme Maria had explained this would occur. And really, it was a good Dom who did discuss these things. "Cuffs are okay. I prefer not to use metal. I have to go back to the real world on Monday and don't want to have to explain any marks. Rope is okay. Zip ties are possible, again, as long as they don't leave any marks."

"Okay, perfect. That's enough for now. I'm not sure how much torture I can fit into a single weekend anyway," Drew said with a wink.

Hannah's eyes were wide as she nodded in acknowledgement, not sure if she was hiding her apprehension very well. She must not have been doing a good job, because Drew took one of her hands in his, holding it reassuringly.

"I will do nothing to hurt you." He smiled wryly. "Well, at least nothing you don't want me to do. I will listen to what you want, and I know what your limits are. Don't be afraid. That's the last thing I want you to feel about me. Understood?"

Her relief must have been palpable as she smiled because Drew leaned over and kissed her gently on the cheek, as if to seal his promise to her. He stood up then and looked down at her questioningly.

"Are you warmer now? And when was the last time you ate? Because I'm starving."

Hannah nodded to indicate she was much warmer, and her stomach growled loudly as if it, too, was responding to Drew's question. They both looked at her stomach and laughed.

"Okay, why don't you get dressed while I make us something to eat in the kitchen? Some Doms prefer their subs stay naked at all times when present. I am not one of them. I prefer a woman in lingerie. Silky, lacy, sexy. When we are here, in this house, I want you dressed as such."

Hannah stood and wrapped the blanket around her, more now for security than warmth. "Yes, Sir."

She was so lucky to have been purchased by a Dominant who seemed to be gentle and caring. If the other man had purchased her instead, her evening probably would have taken a much different turn already. She hoped her first impression of him proved correct.

Chapter Three

Hannah walked into the bedroom and pulled open the drawer of the wardrobe. She gasped at the beautiful colors and fabrics that were revealed. Mostly silks, but some lace, and all in beautiful jewel tones of sapphire, emerald, ruby and onyx. There were more undergarments in the drawer than she could wear in two weeks, let alone two days.

She had no idea what Drew's preferences were, but black was always a classic. There was a gorgeous pair of silk boyshorts, cut high in the back and trimmed with lace. She pulled those on and found the matching bra. The material of the bra was the sheerest silk, again trimmed in lace that matched the panties. The demi cups pushed her breasts up, almost spilling her nipples over the top of the lace. She felt incredibly sexy, sexier than she could have felt naked. There were garters and hose and beautiful, high-heeled shoes, but she decided to keep things simple.

Hannah walked into the kitchen and found Drew at the counter, his back to her, chopping something on a wooden block. He stilled and then turned as she entered. She stopped and waited for his next command.

He had removed his tie and unbuttoned the top few buttons on his dress shirt, revealing dark, curly hair on his chest. His shirtsleeves were rolled up, and he had fastened a makeshift apron around his waist by tucking a dish towel into his belt. He still wore his dress slacks and shoes, but he looked completely at ease in the kitchen. A wicked smile spread across his face as his gaze traveled over the length of her body.

"Scarlett, you look amazing. If I didn't know you were so hungry, I'd throw you up on that counter right now and have my way with you."

Wiping his hands on the towel at his waist, he walked slowly around her and then stopped directly in front of her. He grasped her behind the neck and pulled her to his mouth for a kiss. Soft at first, he swept his tongue against her lips, urging her to open them, and then caressed the inside of her mouth, entwining his tongue with hers. She could taste the bit of lime that had flavored their water, but his kiss was anything but refreshing; it was searingly hot. As the kiss became more urgent, Drew pulled her up against his body, his hand no longer gentle on her neck but firmly on her backside, pressing her into his hardened length. Hannah moaned as she wrapped one hand around his waist, clutching onto his shirt back, while the other fisted in his hair, trying to deepen the kiss consuming her. Their chemistry was electric, like a bolt of lightening had struck them both. Drew broke away from her mouth and slowly trailed a line of wet kisses down her throat, stopping at the base of her neck, nipping lightly before she felt him pull away from her.

Hannah looked up at Drew with hooded eyes, curious why he stopped. Drew grasped her chin, lightly kissed her lips and then pointed to a stool at the counter. "Sit. I need to feed you, and then we can finish that kiss." Hannah looked at the stool, looked at him and then did as he asked. Drew walked back to the counter and returned to cutting a tomato.

"Grilled chicken salad okay?" Drew looked over his shoulder at her.

She nodded yes, but kept silent. He stopped chopping and turned around again.

He looked at her with hard eyes and, his tone short, asked, "Don't you mean, 'Yes, Sir'?"

Hannah flushed red, nodded again and forced out a weak, "Yes, Sir."

"I need you to respond to me verbally, Scarlett. Is that understood?"

"Yes, Sir," Hannah responded quickly, chastising herself for forgetting the most basic of command responses within an hour of being a submissive.

"Good. There will be no misunderstandings this way." He finished chopping all the chicken and vegetables and swept them into a bowl. "Do you have a preference on salad dressing? I was going to use a balsamic, if that's okay?"

"Balsamic is fine, Sir."

Drew poured a small amount of dressing into the salad, grabbed a fork, pulled up a stool and sat in front of her. He was so close that her knees were inside of his spread legs. He punched the fork into the bowl, spearing a piece of chicken and some lettuce before bringing the fork up to her mouth.

"What are you doing?" Hannah asked as she leaned back away from the fork.

Drew frowned in obvious frustration. "I'm going to feed you."

"Why? I can feed myself." Hannah knew she shouldn't question a Dom, but it seemed silly to have someone feed her like a two-year-old.

"Because I want to. It gives me pleasure to take care of your needs." Drew looked down and, after letting out a long breath, said in a sterner tone, g "And if you question me again, I will punish you. Do you understand?"

Hannah nodded and replied meekly, "Yes, Sir."

"Good. Now open up and eat."

Drew raised the fork to her lips, and this time she complied, taking it into her mouth. He slowly slid the fork out, his eyes never leaving hers as he speared more of the salad and again held the fork to her mouth. His eyes still locked on hers, a warmth gathered low in Hannah's belly as it became apparent that feeding her was a much more intimate act than she'd realized. While she chewed, he fed himself bites of the salad, using the same fork. They remained silent throughout, eyes always on each other.

Drew put the fork down after several more bites and brought a glass of ice water to her lips, then tilted it so the chilly water slid over her lips and down her throat. Every action he performed had an undertone of sexuality, of what was sure to come. He fed her several more bites until she shook her head to indicate she was done.

"Had enough?" Drew asked, raising his brow.

"Yes, Sir."

"More water?"

"Yes, Sir."

Drew raised the glass to her lips again. Ice cubes gathered against her lips, creating a damn, causing some of the cold water to spill over the glass, down her neck and onto her breasts. Hannah pulled away quickly, bringing her hands up to her chest to try and stop the spill.

"Stop." Drew stood up quickly, causing Hannah to jump and look up at him timidly under her long lashes.

"I'm sorry, Sir. It was a natural reaction to try and stop the spill."

He let out a slow exhale and then spoke in a firm tone. "Go in the bedroom, kneel beside the bed, and wait."

Hannah looked up at him again apologetically and whispered, "Yes, Sir," before walking quickly into the bedroom and kneeling in position as ordered. She was thoroughly embarrassed, and her body was flushed slightly as her heart beat quickly in her chest. Drew was beautiful, and so far, gentle, and did nothing but offer kindness, but she couldn't seem to follow the simplest of orders to please him. She'd had training—she knew better.

It was that kiss. That hot, wet, 'please throw me up on that counter and fuck me' kiss that had her head rattled. After that kiss, and the way he'd stared longingly at her mouth with every bite he fed her, her body hummed with desire. Who could think straight feeling that way? Not her, that was evident. She needed to gather some control over these desires, or his frustration with her was sure to either lead to some type of punishment, or worse, disinterest.

Drew continued to pace in the kitchen after cleaning up the salad dishes. He knew a maid was available to perform the task, but he needed something to keep his mind busy as he got his emotions under control. Confusion swirled inside of him. He wanted to take Scarlett over his knee and turn her bottom a dark shade of pink, but he also knew she was a new submissive and didn't want to scare her. Trying to control his needs, his desire to do the right thing, wasn't something that came naturally to him.

What was it about this girl that made him so soft, so yielding against her disobedience?

He needed to punish her if he was to teach her to be a good sub and what his expectations were, but damn, the thought of doing anything that might frighten her or scare her away made him hesitate. And besides, weren't these girls supposed to be already trained? Why did he feel so beholden to treat this girl with kid gloves? The last three weeks had been hell for him, and he had been looking forward to fucking his way back to being halfway sane again. Instead, she was making him crazier. He had barely been able to stop himself from throwing her up on the counter and driving himself into her during that kiss, and if he didn't do something to regain some of his control, it would never happen.

"Fuck it." Drew grabbed a large pitcher from the cabinet, filled it with ice and water and walked quickly into the bedroom.

Scarlett was kneeling in position at the corner of the bed, her head down. "Get up, Scarlett."

Scarlett stood up quickly but kept her head down.

"Look at me."

Scarlett complied as he placed the pitcher down on the bedside table next to her.

He stepped closer, grasped her chin lightly and bent down so his face was within inches of hers. "You will do what I ask, when I ask for it, however I ask for it. And you will not question me. Is that understood?"

Scarlett tried to nod, but he held her chin firmly as a reminder to answer him verbally. She refused to meet his gaze but replied, "Yes, Sir."

"Good girl. Now I want you to reach above your head and grasp the bedpost behind you."

Drew didn't move an inch as Scarlett obeyed, the position arching her back, pushing her breasts out, brushing her nipples up against him.

"This is about you learning to obey my commands. Whether you like it or not. Your job is to do what pleases me. Do you understand?"

She responded quietly, "Yes, Sir."

"Good. Remember that."

Drew let go of her chin, took a step away from her and pulled his shirt over his head, exposing his broad, sculpted chest. He worked out almost daily to maintain a fit frame, and the result was a well-defined set of abdominals and a trim waistline. His arms flexed as he grasped the shirt and threw it in a chair across the room. Her eyes raked over his naked torso and darkened in what appeared to be desire. Seeing her reaction brought on a wave of his own desire that further hardened his cock.

Drew grabbed the pitcher and stopped a few inches before her. He leaned into her and whispered in her ear, "I can see how hot this is making you. Let me help cool you off."

He raised the pitcher over her chest, tilted it and slowly let the cold water and ice spill over onto her chest. She gasped in shock at the cold water, sputtering as it splashed up, hit her mouth and ran down her body. She let go of the post in an attempt to wipe the water from her face, but Drew spoke in a commanding tone before she could.

"No, Scarlett. Do not let go of that post." He continued to pour the entire pitcher of water over her chest, causing her already sheer bra to become even more transparent, her chest heaving as she drew in deep gasps in reaction to the cold.

He panted in desire, watching Scarlett cling to the bedpost as she groaned and twisted from the shock of the cold water and ice. He dropped the empty pitcher onto the carpeted floor and grasped her roughly at her sides, bent his head, and pulled one of her nipples into his mouth. He brought one hand to the other breast, pinching the already hard nipple, before sliding the wet fabric of the bra under her breast, freeing it. His mouth was hot as it moved over her cold, wet nipple, sucking and nipping, while he peeled the fabric down below the other breast, uncovering it as well. Using both hands, he pushed her breasts together, sucking on both nipples. Scarlett still held onto the post with a firm grip, not letting go, moaning in pleasure as he continued to relish her breasts.

Drew moved his body up against her, wrapping his arm around her back, pulling her into his hard length. Scarlett reacted by rubbing up and down on him, pressing her core tighter to him.

He pushed her back suddenly and looked down. "No, Scarlett. No relief for you. This is all about what I want. When you please me and learn to obey me, maybe then I'll see what I can do to offer you some relief."

Hannah's eyes widened in disbelief, even though she knew what he was doing. This was torture in its finest form. Her punishment. And she would and could play this game. She had to think about the money at the end of the weekend and what that money would ultimately do for her. She would obey, even if it meant she would be aching for release if he kept this up.

"Yes, Sir."

"Good. Turn around. I want you bent over and your hands back on that post."

Hannah complied and immediately felt Drew against her backside. He ran his hands down her hair, then draped it down over one shoulder, leaving her back bare. He bent over her then, his lower body flush with hers. His soft lips peppered kisses down her back, stopping only when he got to her panties. He hooked his fingers into each side and pulled them down around her ankles, then had her step out of them. His breath caressed up her legs as he slowly worked his way back up her body, then placed a hand on her lower back, pushing it down flatter.

"Open your legs more, and hold the bedpost lower. And don't let go."

Hannah obeyed immediately. "Yes, Sir."

Her entire backside was exposed in this position, but instead of feeling embarrassed, she felt wanton. She curved her back just a bit more as Drew continued his advance up her body, anxious to feel him between her legs now. He was running his tongue up the inside of her thigh, the stubble of his chin lightly scraping her as he got closer to her apex and the growing heat pooling there. She couldn't contain the groan that escaped her as his tongue flicked against her clit in a swiping motion.

He let out a small growl, the vibration stimulating her further. She threw her head back, groaning in frustration, wishing he would fuck her already. Instead, he licked her again and then sucked just the tip of her clit, biting it gently before letting go. She was so close to exploding but didn't want to disobey Drew or worse, disappoint him. She panted desperately, "Sir, I'm going to come if you keep doing that."

Drew stood up, then leaned over her back, his lips at her ear. "Will you obey me now, little one? Do you feel now just how much pleasure I can bring you?"

Hannah whimpered, "Yes, Sir. God, yes. I'll be better."

Drew pulled away and took a couple steps back. His shoes hit the floor with a thunk, then his pants. She was panting with desire for him. She looked over her shoulder and watched as he stroked his hardened cock. His eyes fixed on hers as he stepped forward again, pushing himself flush against her body. He reached down between her legs and stroked her slick pussy with his cock. She pushed herself back against him and down on his cock.

"Tsk, tsk. Remember, Scarlett, this is about what I need right now."

She gasped in surprise as a hard smack suddenly landed on her ass, and stopped her pushing back onto Drew's cock. His very hard, very generous length continued to rub back and forth against her pussy. *How in the world does he expect me not to come when he keeps doing that?*

"Are you ready?" Drew pushed down on the center of her lower back with one hand, causing her ass to arch higher, as he slid his cock into her pussy in one quick thrust. He stayed seated for a moment before grasping her shoulder with his other hand and then began to slide back and forth in a steady motion.

Hannah couldn't help herself—she moaned loudly and pushed back to meet him thrust for thrust. The hand at her shoulder tightened, and the other moved to her waist as Drew surged into her harder and deeper. She was so close. She could feel the build of her orgasm as she grasped tighter onto the bedpost.

"You may *not* come, Scarlett," Drew said between clenched teeth as he continued to slam into her.

"Oh god, Drew, please. I don't think I can stop. Please," she begged.

Drew let go of his grip on her waist and smacked her ass again, this time harder. "No! You may not come!"

She shrieked from the smack and then held her breath and tried to think of anything else but the build of her impending climax. Drew grasped both his hands on her waist now and thrust three more times, hard and deep, before groaning in relief. His hot seed coated her insides with his final push. He held onto her tightly for a moment, his cock jerking slightly at the last of his release, before slowly sliding out of her.

Hannah moaned in frustration as he stepped away, leaving her feeling empty and cool all at once, but without an ounce of relief. Her pussy was hot and wet and pulsing. Not to mention her tingling ass where Drew had smacked her. *He's going to leave me feeling like this? Goddamn bastard.*

Drew pulled her into an upright position, turning her in his arms. He nuzzled the nape of her neck and whispered, "Thank you for that. It was amazing." Then he trailed the softest kisses up her neck until he reached her mouth, kissing her deeply. She was surprised by his sudden tenderness and felt herself soften and mold into him and his kiss. How could he go from one extreme to another so quickly?

He pulled back and pushed the hair away from her face, looking down at her. "Do you need anything? Some water?"

She raised her eyebrows in disbelief and laughed. "Seriously? I think I've had enough water for now."

Drew laughed and pulled her back into his embrace. "Ah yes. I guess so."

He hugged her quickly and then, taking her hand, led her to the adjoining bathroom. "Let's get you cleaned up then, shall we? Do you prefer a bath or a shower?"

"That depends . . . Are you joining me?" she asked coyly.

Drew smiled. "You know what? I think I will join you."

"Then I prefer a bath." Hannah smiled shyly.

Drew bent down and kissed the tip of her nose. "Your wish is my command. Why don't you go find us something to change into after our bath while I start the water?"

"Okay. Do you have something specific you'd like me to wear, Sir?" Hannah fluttered her lashes and looked up at him with her most innocent and demure look, hoping to draw another laugh from him.

He took the bait and grinned. "Oh, I see you're finally getting the hang of this. I suppose I'll have to keep that last fuck in mind in case you forget."

She blushed, but smiled and responded, "I won't forget again, Sir. I promise."

Drew leaned over the very deep, very large oval tub and started running the water to fill it. "I'd prefer you to sleep naked so I can feel you against me whenever I want." Drew raked his gaze down her still-naked body, causing her to blush again at his brazenness.

Feeling emboldened by Drew's approval of her body, Hannah replied in a quiet voice, "I can do naked. If it means being up against you again."

She thought she saw a spark of desire in Drew's eyes before he turned and started walking back toward the bedroom. "I'll go get us something to drink while the water is running. There are usually several types of bath salts and bubbles under the sink if you'd like to pick something out and add it to the tub."

"Okay, thank you, Sir."

She used the toilet and cleaned herself up a bit. It was strange to think of having sex with a relative stranger and not having to discuss protection. When she'd become an employee of the club, her blood had been tested for sexually transmitted diseases. She'd also had to agree to birth control and regular testing to confirm she stayed clean.

She found a bottle of ginger-scented bubble bath and added it to the running water. Once the tub was about half full, she decided to climb in and wait for Drew to return. Before stepping in, she wound her long hair up into a bun and knotted it at the top of her head. The tub was so deep that it had an actual step around half the inside perimeter to use.

She slowly lowered herself into the hot, bubbly water. The heat felt so good against her skin, a stark contrast from the ice-water shower she'd just endured, causing her to sigh in pleasure. When the hot water hit her core, it stung a moment from the aggressive fucking she'd just received, but after a moment in the water, she felt nothing but soothed. Hannah scooted herself up against the far side of the tub wall, leaned back and let herself relax.

Still naked, Drew walked in a moment later, carrying two glasses of white wine, and set them on the ledge of the tub. She couldn't help but admire him, her eyes taking in his entire body.

"I thought this might be refreshing in the tub. How's the water?"

Hannah reached across the tub to take a glass of the wine. "It's divine. Are you coming in?"

Instead of answering, Drew stepped into the tub, grabbed the other glass and sat down in the water across from her. His legs were long and instead of moving them to the side, he entwined them with hers.

"What scent did you choose for the bubbles? I love it."

"It's ginger. I was so happy when I saw it. It's one of my absolute favorite scents. I'm glad you like it as well."

Drew nodded. "I do."

There was silence between them then, but Drew didn't take his eyes off of her. "You're quite beautiful, Scarlett."

Hannah blushed at the compliment. "Thank you. You're quite beautiful too. But I'm sure you're aware of that already."

Drew smiled. "Yes, well, I suppose I've been called handsome. Tall, dark and mysterious. Rich always helps, of course." He looked down into the water and then back up at her. "But I don't think I've been called beautiful."

She took another sip of her wine and frowned slightly. "Well, I think you're beautiful. I don't think I've ever seen or been with a man as beautiful as you. I really don't think I want you to put your clothes back on this weekend."

Drew threw his head back and laughed. "Well, you're in luck, because I don't think I want you to put your clothes back on all weekend either."

She smiled broadly, raising her eyebrows in a teasing fashion. "Then I guess I don't have to ask what we'll be doing for the rest of the weekend."

He smiled back. "Tell me more about yourself. Are you a brand new submissive or just new to Baton Timide?"

She looked down into the water before answering. She had been warned by Domme Maria to only expose what she really needed to about herself and to try and not get overly personal with the Doms. Hannah didn't want to cross that line of course, but she also knew they needed some personal engagement between each other. She just wanted to make sure it wasn't too much.

"This is my first time. At Baton Timide or anywhere. Is it that obvious?" she asked nervously.

"No. Well, maybe a little." He sipped his wine, slowly brushing his legs up and down hers, and shrugged. "We've only just started out, but it seemed like you were a bit nervous up on the stage at the auction, so I assumed you were new, and then of course Domme Maria confirmed you were at least new to the club."

Hannah looked down at the water as she answered timidly, "Yes, I was definitely nervous. Then excited, and then nervous again when I wondered who had bid on me."

She glanced up at him then, meeting his eyes before continuing, "And then excited again when I discovered it was you."

He put his wineglass down on the edge of the tub and sat upright. "Come here, come closer to me. Let me wash your back."

She untangled her legs from his and scooted closer. He took her wineglass and put it on the edge of the tub next to his. He grabbed a washcloth, squirted some body wash on it and started to rub slow, small circles over her back. She sighed, her body relaxing totally. When her entire back had been washed and rinsed, he pulled her between his legs, her back now resting against his chest.

She wiggled for a moment and then stopped. "Your chest hair feels ticklish against my back."

"I'd offer to shave it for you, but seeing how we're only spending the weekend together . . ."

"No, don't shave it. I like it. It's sexy when it peeks through your shirt."

Drew smiled at her admission and began to wash her front. He started at her neck, continued over her breasts, then down her stomach, ending between her legs. As his fingers brushed lightly over her clit, she gasped, her legs opening wider for him.

Drew let the washcloth drop into the water, and continued to caress her. Using both hands, he massaged each breast. Hannah moaned and pushed them higher into his hands. Her nipples elongated as he pinched and pulled them. As his cock hardened against her backside, she rocked back into his length. He hissed and snaked one of his hands down her stomach, into the water and over her pussy, finding her sensitive nub. She cried out as her body hitched out of the water from his touch.

"Do you like that, little one?" Drew whispered in her ear and began licking and sucking down the length of her neck.

She leaned her head back and to the side to give him better access as she moaned a husky, "Yes." Her entire body was pulsing with desire, aching to feel his touch on her everywhere and anywhere.

He whispered in her ear again, "Turn around and sit on me. It's your turn now."

Hannah rose up so quickly that water sloshed over the sides and knocked one of the wine glasses into the tub as she turned around.

Drew chuckled and held her by the waist as she slowly lowered herself back into the water, over him. "Anxious, are we?"

She locked her eyes with his, bringing her head down to his, her lips to his, and breathed, "Yes," before kissing him deeply, tasting the wine on his lips.

He pulled her in closer with a hand at her nape, thrusting his tongue in her mouth, stealing her breath away. With the other hand, he held his cock and guided it into her as she lowered herself onto him. As she became fully seated, a groan rolled out of her mouth and into his.

He was big, not just in length but in girth as well, and sitting on him like this filled her differently than when he took her from behind. She felt so full as the throbbing of her pussy clenched around his cock, getting used to its size.

Drew pulled away from her mouth, kissing a trail to her ear before commanding, "Ride me, Scarlett. It's all about you now." And then he continued kissing down her neck, lightly nipping her along the way, fueling her desire even further.

Hannah's head fell against his as she began to rock back and forth, sliding his cock in and out, holding onto his shoulders to help her move. Her clit was rubbing along his shaft every time she slid forward, and she didn't know how long she could last.

"Drew, I'm going to come," she breathed out heavily as she continued to ride him, head still against his. She increased her speed, throwing her head back, her long hair falling out of its makeshift bun and grazing the top of her arched ass, water sloshing over the edge of the tub.

Drew started to move with her, pumping his cock into Scarlett harder, pushing her to go faster. The sight of her on top of him, head thrown back, moaning in pleasure, was one of the sexiest things he had ever seen. He fisted her loose hair in his hand and pushed Scarlett down harder on his cock while he thrust up. He felt the moment she came as her pussy tightened around him, surrounding him in warmth. He loosened his grip on her and nuzzled his nose into her hair. She smelled like fresh flowers in the spring.

"So beautiful." He sighed, then kissed her lips. She began to rise and lift herself off him, but he pulled her back onto his still-hard cock and held her in his arms. "Stay like this for a minute. I just want to feel you."

Scarlett sank back onto him and trailed soft kisses down his neck before resting her head there. He wrapped his arms around her waist, pulling her tighter for a moment before relaxing. She lifted her head up off his shoulder and turned her face to his. He met her gaze and then kissed her gently on the mouth. Pulling away, he traced his finger down her cheek and over her lips. She flicked her tongue out and used it to guide his finger into her mouth. Closing her lips around it, she sucked hard, staring down at him between her lashes. Drew sucked in his breath as he rocked his hips, pushing his cock a little deeper inside her.

He rested his forehead against hers and, in a strained voice, whispered, "What are you trying to do to me, Scarlett?"

He pulled his finger out of her mouth with a pop and replaced it with his tongue. As the kiss became more heated, a need to possess her further swept through him.

Drew pulled his lips from hers and grasped the edge of the tub with one hand. "Wrap your legs around me and hold on."

Holding on to the edge of the tub, he pushed and stood up, Scarlett wrapped around him tightly. He folded both arms around her after he stepped out of the tub and walked into the shower, turning it on quickly. Freezing-cold water rained down, causing Scarlett to gasp and clutch him tighter. Drew wasted no time pushing her up against the shower wall and driving into her with need.

Scarlett's arms cinched more tightly around him as she met him thrust for thrust. Moans of pleasure escaped her mouth each time he drove his cock into her, making him even harder. He braced one hand up against the shower wall so he could push even deeper into her.

She clung to him and panted out between thrusts, "Drew, I'm going to come again."

Hearing his name come moaning from her lips caused his balls to tighten and his own release to reach its peak. "Then come, let me feel you again."

With Scarlett clutching his shoulders and her legs wrapped tightly around his waist, he thrust his hips into her hard, hand still braced on the wall. Her muscles began to tighten around him in orgasm. He lowered his head to her shoulder and bit hard as they both yelled out their release.

He slowly lowered Scarlett's legs to the floor but continued to hold her close. He bent over her and, bringing his lips to hers, kissed her lightly. He traced his nose softly across her cheek and whispered into her ear, "You are amazing." Her cheeks rose in a smile before she kissed him back warmly.

They slowly pulled apart as he turned to adjust the water to a warmer temperature. Without saying a word, he took a washcloth and, applying soap, carefully washed and rinsed her off before doing the same to himself. He shut the water off, stepped out, grabbed a towel and wrapped it around her tenderly.

Scarlett looked at herself in the mirror, running her fingers over the bite mark he had left on her shoulder. Her eyes met his in the mirror questioningly. "You bit me?"

He'd forgotten he'd even done that. It wasn't something he ever remembered doing before, but with her, when he came, something had possessed him. A need to mark her as his. He wasn't even sure how to explain it.

He stepped closer and grazed his fingers lightly over the bite mark. "I'm sorry. Does it hurt?"

She shook her head in response. "Not really. I was just surprised."

Little did she know that he was too. He pulled some antiseptic ointment out of one of the drawers. "Let me put some of this on it. It will help quicken the healing."

He didn't want to apologize again, because deep down, as hard as it was for him to admit it, he liked seeing his mark on her. *Jesus, am I turning into some kind of animal?* After applying the ointment, he kissed the top of her head and turned her toward the bedroom.

"Go ahead and climb into bed. I'll just clean up a bit in here and join you."

"We'll sleep in the same bed then?"

In her training, Scarlett had probably been made aware that Doms generally didn't sleep in the same bed as their submissives. And normally, that was the case with him as well. But since he'd first seen her on that stage this evening, he'd felt an inexplicable urge to be near her.

"Yes, I'd like that, if you would?" He looked questioningly at her.

"Yes, I'd like that too." She reached up on her tiptoes and kissed him before walking away.

He watched as she left the bathroom, still wrapped in her towel, hair loose and damp down her back. Then he rinsed the tub and gathered the wineglasses. As he entered the bedroom, his heart stopped at the sight before him: Scarlett, eyes closed, her long, golden hair spread out around her face on the pillow, her cheeks flushed, and her lips pink and soft as she slept.

She took his breath away. He had only spent a few hours with her, and already it felt like more. It wasn't just that she was beautiful. He'd been with many beautiful girls, and they had all been eager to please him. Perhaps it was her innocence? He wasn't sure. He continued to stare down at her while contemplating. Was there such a thing as love at first sight? He shook his head at the absurdity of his own thoughts. He definitely didn't live in a land of fairy tales, but he couldn't deny the possessive feelings he was having.

He put the wineglasses down on the bedside table, turned out the lights, climbed in beside her and pulled her into his arms. She muttered something unintelligible in her sleep and then settled down. She was like a newborn kitten cuddled up against him. He listened to the soft, steady cadence of her breathing, and felt the satin of her skin against his, and soon was sound asleep as well.

Chapter Four

Drew woke around six and was surprised to find himself wrapped around Scarlett. It was an intimacy he hadn't experienced since his divorce four years ago. Waking up in bed with his wife and spending mornings with her had been one of the happier parts of his marriage. Until the day he'd come home early from a business trip to find her in that same bed with another man. She'd blamed it on him, of course. Saying he'd betrayed her first when she realized his business was like a mistress and would always come first. Perhaps she'd been right. Owning and running a billion-dollar hotel chain required much of his time, but she'd known that when she'd married him. He had always invited her to attend all of his business trips with him, but after only a few trips, she'd begun refusing, claiming she had her own schedule to keep.

After the divorce, he'd been introduced to the club by a friend. He'd become instantly intrigued and found that the club allowed him to maintain a level of control over relationships that real life didn't allow. He wouldn't or couldn't even claim to be a full-time dominant. He enjoyed the control and light punishment his role encompassed, but it was something he only maintained in the bedroom—and as a convenience to help maintain order in his world. He had no time to deal with the complications that came with feelings or commitment.

Or at least, that's what he had thought before he'd laid eyes on Scarlett last night.

He disentangled himself as gently as he could from her and sat up on the edge of the bed. He looked over his shoulder at her sleeping form and wondered again what the fuck she was doing to him. Her hands were resting together in prayer formation against her face, her thick eyelashes brushing against her cheekbones, her full lips parted slightly as she breathed. It was very tempting to climb back in that bed and wake her in a way he was sure would be satisfying to both of them, but he needed a little space.

He rose and quietly walked to the walk-in master closet that housed his clothes. He dressed quickly, pulling on his jogging clothes before exiting the house, grabbing his iPod on the way. It was still dark out, so he stood on the porch for a moment to let his eyes adjust to the light.

September had arrived, but the early morning air was chillier than he had anticipated. He contemplated going back inside to grab a sweatshirt but didn't want to risk waking Scarlett. He would warm up once he started running. He popped his ear buds in and selected his favorite playlist for a run: Bon Jovi's *Slippery When Wet*. His older brother had given him the CD when he was younger, proclaiming it was the best album ever written. Drew didn't know if he would go that far, but it was a classic, and the familiar songs always relaxed him while running. The songs also had some great memories associated with them, so it remained a permanent fixture on his iPod.

His eyes adjusted to the light as he followed the sidewalk out to the road. He started jogging at a slow pace until his muscles warmed up and then worked his way up to a steady gait through the first song on the album, "Let it Rock."

Each breath he took left his body in a puff of white fog, and he could feel the echo of each foot hitting the pavement. By the third song on the album, "Livin' on a Prayer," he had reached his stride, and his muscles stretched a bit as he increased to a run. He tried to run five or six miles every morning. Not only for the health benefits, but to keep his head clear. This morning though, he had only one thought on his mind, and that was Scarlett.

His mind raced, trying to determine how to handle her when he returned to the bungalow. Maybe it would be best to become truly dominant for the rest of the weekend and dispense with any of the casual pleasantries they had so thoroughly enjoyed last night. It would eliminate any of the personal details and emotions she seemed to be invoking within him thus far. He still had to decide whether or not he wanted her to accompany him to the fundraiser he was scheduled to attend that evening. Normally he wouldn't leave the club during a weekend stay, but it was for his brother's organization, and he'd promised Benny he would be there.

Drew was running at a hard pace now, covering almost a mile every seven minutes or so. He'd lost track of how long he'd been running and was surprised to look at his watch and discover he'd been at it almost an hour. He slowed down to a light jog and cut across the woods to bring him closer to the bungalow without having to backtrack.

It was lighter now that the sun had risen and the temperature had warmed, so the shade from the trees was welcome. When he came out of the other side of the woods, he realized he was only about a mile from the bungalow and decided to walk the rest of the way to cool his muscles down.

Inside the bungalow, all the lights were still off and the house was silent. Scarlett must still be sleeping. He walked into the second bedroom and into its accompanying bathroom and stripped out of his workout clothes. He turned on the shower and stepped in to wash off the sweat from his run. As the water ran over him, rinsing him clean, he was reminded of the shower he and Scarlett had taken the night before. He recalled how good she'd felt wrapped around his body, him buried deep inside her as she moaned his name. The memory stirred his blood and hardened his cock. He shut the water off, stepped out of the stall and grabbed a towel off the rack. He quickly dried himself off and, staying naked, walked into the master bedroom, where Scarlett was still sleeping. Here, now, he needed to treat Scarlett as his submissive if he had any hope of walking away from her at the end of this weekend.

He stood beside the bed, naked, his cock growing harder at the sight of her, and jostled the bed with his knee. "Scarlett, wake up."

Hannah felt the bed shake and rolled over, slowly opening her eyes. She blinked a few times, trying to wake herself up. She rose up on her elbows to find Drew standing over her, naked.

Before she even had time to form a thought, he spoke roughly to her. "Get on your hands and knees, facing me."

She paused, momentarily shocked by his tone and request.

He lunged forward, grabbing a handful of her hair painfully as he bent toward her and seethed into her ear, "What did I tell you about repeating myself?"

As he let go and straightened to his full height, she quickly scooted onto her hands and knees and faced him. He was tall, so his cock, hard and jutting, was right in her face. She looked up at him, unsure of what he wanted her to do next.

"Open your mouth."

Now she knew. But still she hesitated. Before she could react, a hard smack rained down on her ass. She instinctively lowered her ass away from his smack while looking sheepishly up at him.

"I told you I would punish you if you hesitated again." He stared down, his eyes hard and dilated with lust. "Open your mouth. *Now.*"

This time, she didn't hesitate. Her mouth opened instantly. In the same instant, Drew took a step forward and, gripping his cock, led it to her mouth. She closed her lips around it, raising her hands up off the bed to grasp him.

"No," he commanded. "Hands on the bed."

Hands midway to his shaft, she froze. He, however, didn't hesitate and smacked her ass again, not once but three times, and they weren't gentle. The quick gasp she took in surprise sucked his cock deeper into her mouth, and he hissed in response. She returned her hands to the bed, her eyes still raised in question.

"I am going to fuck your mouth now, Scarlett. And since I can't have the pleasure of coming in your mouth, when I'm ready, I'm going to fuck your beautiful pussy."

He took a fistful of her hair in one hand and, pulling it, used it to guide her mouth back and forth over his cock in a slow, agonizing rhythm.

She should feel humiliated by this, but instead, adrenaline coursed through her body, going straight to her core, which quickly dampened from the excitement. She wrapped her mouth tighter around Drew's cock as he slowly entered her mouth. She sucked on him hard, bringing him deep into her mouth, and then pressed her tongue against the bottom of his hardened ridge. When he pulled almost entirely out of her mouth, she swirled her tongue around the tip and then sucked again, bringing him back deep inside. His head was thrown back, his mouth open in an O as he let out a low, guttural moan.

His grip on her hair tightened with each thrust as he began pushing his cock in harder and faster. Just as her mouth started to ache and she worried he might come, he pulled away and used the grip on her hair to yank her head all the way back, forcing her to look up at him.

"Now, turn around, Scarlett. I want your elbows on the mattress and your ass in the air."

When he released her hair, she instantly turned, fell onto her elbows and thrust her ass up. His finger grazed her wet pussy, and she jerked in response.

"Look how wet you are." He hummed appreciatively as he ran his finger up and down her pussy. "You like sucking my cock?"

"Yes." Hannah flinched as she felt a hard smack on her ass. *Shit! That hurt.* She had to remember to answer immediately.

"Yes? Yes, what?"

"Yes, Sir. Yes, I like sucking your cock, Sir." She spoke quickly, but softly.

He rubbed her ass where he had smacked it, just beyond where the ache in her pussy was now throbbing with need.

"Good girl. I liked you sucking my cock. Next time maybe you'll reconsider taking everything my cock has to offer."

She wasn't sure what to say, but she didn't want to get spanked again. To be safe, she responded, "Yes, Sir."

"Now I'm going to fuck you." Drew began stroking her pussy again with his finger, running it up and down her clit, spreading her juices, staying a breath away from her sensitive nub. "And you will not come."

At that statement, Drew brought his cock to her entrance and drove into her in one thrust, her body jerking forward. And he kept thrusting into her. She had to push herself down harder into the bed on her elbows and shove her ass back to keep up with the punishing movements. His cock, rock hard, was hitting her in just the right place every time he pushed into her and she wasn't sure if she was going to be able to hold back from having an orgasm. As if he could read her mind, Drew grabbed a fistful of her hair and, dragging her head back so she could see his face, said through gritted teeth, "Do not come."

"Yes, S-sir," she stammered.

Drew released her hair, grabbed her hips roughly with both hands and slammed into her even harder. She moaned in pleasure, in frustration, in fear, before he thrust one final time, grunting loudly as he came. She could feel his release explode inside her and she had to bite down on her lip, hard, and concentrate with every ounce of her being to keep her orgasm at bay.

Drew's harsh breathing decreased as he softened inside her. As he slid out of her, he released the firm hold he'd had on her hips and then took a step away. His seed slid out of her and down the inside of her leg. She didn't dare move an inch without his consent for fear of another spanking.

"You can relax." Drew spoke quietly, but authoritatively from behind her.

She responded immediately with a quiet, "Yes, Sir," and then rolled onto her side, pulling the covers up over her body. Drew stood looking down at her for several moments before shaking his head and walking away.

"Scarlett, please shower and dress. When you're done, meet me in the kitchen. I'd like breakfast." As he reached the doorway, he turned back with one final command. "Do not touch yourself or offer yourself any relief."

She lay in the bed for just a moment after he left and then quickly got up. She was a mix of emotions. Frustration being at the top of the list. The throbbing at her core needed attention, and knowing she couldn't provide it—and not knowing when she would actually get some relief—did nothing but inflame her. She knew she had no right to be angry. This is what Drew had paid for. She was his to do with as he pleased.

She turned the shower on, keeping the water more cold than hot in an attempt to quench some of the heat coursing through her. She stepped in and let the water run over her body before pulling her hands through her long hair, getting it wet enough to wash. As she shampooed and conditioned her hair, her thoughts went back to Drew's behavior from last night and how it contrasted with his behavior this morning. Perhaps he'd wanted to ease her nerves last night, but today, it was game on? Last night seemed to be more than that, but how would she know? This was her first time, and one of the most important things Domme Maria had instilled in all the trainees was to keep their emotions in check. This was a job and nothing more and she needed to remember that. No matter how well Drew could fuck.

She finished her shower quickly, stepped out of the stall and dried off. She found some lotions in the vanity and, picking one blindly, applied it liberally to her body, spending a little extra time on her smarting bottom. She stepped into the bedroom and opened the drawers, viewing the many lingerie sets, trying to determine which one Drew would like. Since she was going to be cooking, practical would be smart. Boyshorts were a more appropriate choice, than say, a thong. She slipped on a beautifully colored lilac set that would be perfect.

She wasn't quite sure what to do with her hair. Blow-drying it would take another fifteen minutes and she didn't want to chance angering Drew if he was already sitting in the kitchen, waiting for her. Perhaps the easiest thing would be to brush it and then wind it up in a messy bun on top of her head. She needed it out of her way anyway for cooking. Hoping Drew would be happy with her presentation, she made her way out to the kitchen.

Drew was sitting at the kitchen table, hair still wet and disheveled from his shower, holding a cup of coffee and a paper spread out before him. He wore a pair of faded jeans and a white T-shirt. She couldn't help think, for just a fleeting second, that it felt like a normal morning in any other relationship. Except for her scantily dressed form, and her stinging bottom of course.

Fuck. Fuck. Fuck. He was so fucked. All he'd wanted to do when she'd rolled off her knees and under the covers was to crawl in there and cradle her in his arms. He'd wanted to stroke her hair, cover her in kisses and then taste her sweet pussy, giving her the satisfaction she'd so willingly given him. He'd never felt this way about any of the subs he'd had before. He'd gone in there to get some of his control back, to fully dominate her, to impose order on the emotions she was triggering. *What the fuck is she doing to me? 'Cause that definitely didn't go as planned.* Drew turned the shower on as cold as he could make it and stepped inside, hoping it would shock some fucking sense back into him.

After showering, (again), dressed and barefoot, he made his way into the kitchen to fix a pot of coffee. He could still hear the shower running in the other bedroom and wondered if he should check to make sure she was okay. *No.* He'd better give himself a bit more space before seeing her again. The coffee finished brewing, so he poured himself a cup and sat at the table to read the paper that must have been dropped off at some point.

Several moments later, the patter of her footsteps drew his attention as Scarlett entered the room. She was wearing some delectable lace in a purple color that was doing nothing to tamp down the desire he was already struggling with. He focused his eyes back on his paper, trying to remain aloof, and gestured to the counter.

"There's coffee made if you would like a cup."

"Thank you, Sir." She stood rooted in place for a moment before walking over with soft, quick steps to the counter and pouring herself a cup of coffee. He'd left the cream and sugar on the counter, and she added a bit of each to her cup.

"Sir, would you like more coffee?" She raised the pot in question.

He glanced up briefly before looking back down at his paper. "Yes, and a little cream, please."

He was trying very hard to pretend the paper had his full attention but he wasn't sure she was buying it. She walked over, filled his cup and then added a bit of cream.

"Thank you." He took a sip. Without looking up at her, he said, "I'd like an egg-white omelet with tomatoes and cheese, please."

Scarlett stood with the pot suspended midair, hesitating yet again, something obviously on her mind. If only he knew what.

Drew raised an eyebrow and instead of asking her what she was thinking responded casually, "Really, Scarlett? Is it that hard to follow an order?"

"No, Sir. Sorry, Sir. Do you want toast or any meat with your eggs?" She quickly replaced the pot and walked over to the fridge to gather the ingredients needed for his breakfast.

"No toast, no meat." Drew turned the page of the paper he was supposedly reading and continued to ignore her as she went about making his breakfast. Jesus Christ, her ass looked fucking edible in that lace. What he really wanted to do was throw her up on the table and eat *her* for breakfast. He silently cursed himself for being such a cold prick, but he needed to get a grip on his emotions.

Scarlett's body language and ever-expressive face screamed frustration. As he continued the pretense of reading the paper, he covertly watched as she reached for a pan out of one of the lower cupboards. He couldn't help but notice that she bent at the waist and pointed her delectable ass right in his line of vision. Watching her try to push up her breasts while nonchalantly beat the eggs for his omelet had him raising the paper up to cover his smile. When he lowered the paper again, she stuck her ass out, making sure it swayed each time she adjusted the omelet in the pan.

Drew shifted in his seat, trying to gain some control over his growing erection, and knew Scarlett was teasing him. Every action she performed resulted in some kind of ass or breast thrust. And damn if it wasn't working. He was ready to bend her over the counter, rip that lace off and fuck that ass until she learned who was boss. But then she really would be the winner of this little game she was playing, and there was no way he was letting that happen. After this display, he had much bigger plans for that ass, and it would be on his terms, not hers.

Scarlett placed his breakfast before him—bending deeply, of course. "Can I get you anything else, Sir?"

He chuckled at her seductive efforts. "No, thank you. Please make yourself something to eat though."

"I'm not really much of a breakfast eater, Sir."

He looked at her sternly. "You will eat breakfast when you are with me. I have plans for you this morning, and you will need the nourishment."

She flushed at the meaning of his words and then answered, "Yes, Sir." He turned his attention toward his omelet as she walked to the fridge and took more items out.

A few minutes later, he looked up from his breakfast and frowned at Scarlett standing motionless in the center of the room. "What's wrong?"

"Sir, am I allowed to sit with you?"

He was taken aback by her need to ask the question. "Of course." He got up and pulled out a chair for her, then helped her to sit.

"Thank you, Sir. May I eat, or will you be feeding me again?"

Drew tilted his head at her question, surprised at how quickly her behavior had altered. "You may feed yourself, Scarlett. Thank you for asking."

He continued to watch her and realized she was looking for some kind of praise for her actions. She wanted to please him. She wanted to know that he was pleased. She was more submissive by nature than even she may have known. This alone pleased him more than any ass thrust she'd given him.

Hannah began eating. *Why am I doing this again?* She was worrying a little bit too much about what Drew thought of her. As a submissive, her goal was to try and physically please him, but she was alarmed to discover that she was actually starting to really care about how or what he was feeling. When she made him laugh, her heart soared in elation. And the way he'd held her as they'd slept last night had felt more intimate than some relationships she'd had with past lovers. Her feelings were starting to confuse her.

Although the sex was pretty damn amazing, this was all about the bottom line. She was fooling herself if she thought she was going to run away with the rich playboy at the end of this weekend. Buying the shop—*her* shop—was going to give her the independence and security she hadn't felt in years. That was why she was here. This wasn't just about her.

Only one of her friends knew what she was actually doing this weekend. She'd had to confide in at least one person. Her best friend Tammy not only understood but would be there to catch her if she fell. She had tried to get a bridge loan from the bank to cover the down payment for the shop, but she couldn't meet all of their strict requirements. And what normal person has an extra thirty grand around for someone to borrow?

She looked up from her yogurt to find Drew staring intently at her. She knew why she was here, but what about him? What went on in that moody mind of his, and what made a man like him purchase sex? He was amazingly good-looking and obviously had money, so it would probably be safe to assume he had his choice of women.

Drew raised an eyebrow as she continued to stare at him. "What's on your mind?"

She blushed crimson at being called out on her bold appraisal. "Um, just wondering what we'll be doing today, Sir?"

Drew rose and circled behind her, removing the clip holding her hair up. He ran his fingers through her still-damp hair, trying to straighten it down her back. "I like your hair down. Please leave it this way unless I instruct otherwise."

"Yes, Sir. I was only trying to save time by not drying it and I threw it up instead," she defended.

He still stood behind her, slowly caressing his fingers through her hair. She loved the feel of his touch. She wanted to lean back into it but was nervous at his sudden sternness again. "I appreciate that you were trying to be efficient. Down from now on though."

She nodded. "Yes, Sir."

He moved beside her again, looking down at her. She didn't know how to read him yet and wasn't sure what the look in his eye meant. "I want you down in the playroom in position in five minutes. Do you know where it's located?"

She nodded. "Yes, Sir, I know where it is."

"Good. Five minutes." Drew turned and started walking out of the room, then stopped. "And, Scarlett? Be naked."

Chapter Five

Hannah squeaked out a, "Yes, Sir!" before quickly getting up from her chair and following him out of the kitchen. He turned left into the second bedroom, and she turned right, opposite the entryway, going through a doorway that led down to the playroom. Her training session had occurred in a similar bungalow, and she knew that a playroom was housed in the basement of each residence on the property.

Her heart started beating heavily as she descended the stairs down to the playroom. The room was warm, in both temperature and color. The floor was made up of honey-colored hardwood, and beautifully colored Oriental rugs were scattered throughout the room. The playroom was large, encompassing in one room what the entire first-floor space shared with five rooms. In the farthest corner of the room, an enormous bed was covered in a rich, blue velvet sheets. Of course the bed had four high posts, one at each corner, but unlike other bedposts, these had ornate rings attached for tethering. The headboard also had several rings across its front for similar purposes.

Directly in the center of the room lay a table, a bit higher than a standard table, but as long and wide. But this table had a layer of brown leather padding and was studded with rings at certain points.

In the opposite corner of the room from the bed, a large wooden cross dominated the wall: a St. Andrew's Cross.

The ceiling was crisscrossed by a suspension system that could be used for various swings, attachments or straps. The room also had a spanking bench, several other stools and smaller wooden chairs. An elegant brown leather couch sat against a wall next to the bed. Straps, belts, floggers, canes and other tools for implementing pain and punishment decorated an entire sidewall, hanging for a Dom's use. Near the stairway, a wooden cabinet with drawers and doors of different sizes housed other "tools" of the trade.

Hannah removed the lace garments she was wearing and placed them neatly on top of the cabinet. She moved to one of the Oriental rugs strategically placed near the bottom of the stairs and kneeled in her submissive position. She blew air slowly of her mouth, trying to calm her rapid breathing over the anticipation she was feeling. In this place, a Master could truly have his every desire, but the cost could be at the expense of her breaking point. And she had no idea what or where that point was. At least her first real experience with a Dominant would be at Drew's hands. She already felt she could trust him, that he wouldn't hurt her. On the heels of that thought, the door above opened, and footsteps descended the stairs.

Blood rushed through her as her adrenaline spiked and her body flushed a dark pink. Surely Drew would hear, if not see, her pulse beating so rapidly. His bare feet appeared in front of her, and then his hand was on her head, sliding under her chin and raising it. She turned her gaze up to meet his, lust evident in his dark eyes.

"Are you nervous, Scarlett?" he asked quietly.

"Yes, Sir. A little." Her voice was barely above a whisper.

"Good." He let go of her chin but still stood above her. "You should be a little nervous. After all, it's your first time. But, tell me, are you afraid?"

She shook her head while continuing to look up at Drew. "No, Sir. I'm not afraid of you."

He smiled leisurely down at her. "Good. I don't want you to ever be afraid of me. I won't hurt you. Do you remember your safe word?"

He isn't going to hurt me, but he wants to make sure I remember my safe word? Hannah gulped before replying, "Yellow if I'm scared; ghost if I want you to stop."

He leaned down and brushed a kiss lightly against her lips before whispering against them, "Good girl. Don't worry, you won't need them. If I have my way, the only thing you'll be screaming is my name."

A small gasp of surprise escaped her mouth as he quickly rose and approached the cabinet near the stairs. He opened several drawers, pulling various things out and placing them next to her underwear on top of the cabinet before returning to her. Something was in his hand—what was it? As if he had read her thoughts, he flashed her the elastic he was holding before walking behind her.

He ran his hands slowly down her still-damp hair and gathered it in a ponytail at the base of her head. Her constrained hair bobbed up and down as he bound it with the elastic. "As much as I love your hair loose and free down your naked back, I'm going to pull it back while we are in here. I don't want it to get caught in anything."

"Yes, Sir."

Drew's hand ran lightly over the long mane of the tail, his fingertips grazing her naked back with each downward stroke. "Do you know what you remind me of, Scarlett?"

"No, Sir."

"A little kitten. A bit fierce and petulant when it's not under its mother's paw. A kitten will bite and tease its mother's tail, or run away from its mother's call. But as soon as the kitten is hungry or is back under its mother's paw, it is sweet and complying. Do you know what I'm referring to, Scarlett?"

She shook her head again. "No, Sir, I don't understand."

He grasped Hannah's ponytail and, pulling it gently, motioned for her to rise. He took her hand and led her to the padded table in the center of the room. "Stay here."

He continued speaking as he walked back to the cabinet and pulled several more items from one of the drawers. "This morning, making my breakfast, shaking and pointing your delectable ass at me. Teasing me. Playing with me like a little kitten."

She turned crimson at the mention of her actions less than a half hour earlier. She was definitely going to be punished. "But, Sir—"

Drew lifted his hand abruptly. "Did I say you could speak?"

"No, Sir. I'm sorry, Sir." She looked down at the floor quickly, her gaze not meeting his.

"I'm quite sure you are sorry now, my little kitten."

He gathered all the items he had removed and walked slowly back to her side. He placed them on the table, in clear view, as if to give her an idea of what was about to happen. One by one, he lined up four silk straps in a deep blue color, a vibrator, a tube of lubricant and a medium-sized butt plug. Her eyes widened in shock before flying up to meet Drew's. He was looking down at her with a wicked grin on his face, a feral look in his eyes.

"And, Scarlett, do you know why little kittens tease like this?" He stood directly in front of her now and removed his T-shirt, revealing his sculpted chest. Her eyes trailed down his body and she clenched her fists tightly to keep her fingers from raking through the downy hair that covered his muscular chest.

She stammered, "S-s-sir?"

Making her feel like his prey, Drew walked slowly around her in a circle, then leaned in close, lips brushing up against her ear. "Because they want attention."

His hand brushed slowly down her arm until he reached her hand, pulling her tenderly to the front of the padded table. He guided her up, sliding her back about a foot and then pushing her torso down flat.

Her heart beat wildly as he grabbed each of her ankles and pulled them to the edge, and she let out a short, startled cry. He took one of the blue silk ribbons and began winding it around her right ankle. His fingertips felt like hot bolts of electricity each time he grazed her skin, the heat slowly trailing up her legs and throughout her body. He was barely touching her, and already her desire for him was building to a burn.

"Was there something that warranted my attention this morning, little kitten, that I didn't respond to?" Drew took the ends of the blue silk he'd wrapped around her ankle and secured them to one of the rings at the corner of the table. The silk felt tight as he pulled it taut, but soft and pliant, so she wasn't as scared as she'd expected at being constrained.

She knew exactly why she had teased him, but she wasn't going to admit it to him. "Sir, I was simply trying to make you breakfast."

He clucked his tongue in disapproval as he took another one of the silk ties and began wrapping it around her left ankle. "Oh, Scarlett. Shame on you. Do you really think you can fool me? I'll give you one more chance, and if you don't answer honestly, after I'm done with you here, we'll visit the spanking bench."

She blew out an exasperated breath and shakily responded, "Sir, I didn't like being treated like the help. You're hot, then cold, and it's confusing. I guess I was trying to act the part I thought you wanted." Her cheeks flamed in embarrassment, and Drew stopped tying the binding he had been working on.

Drew ran his hand through his hair in frustration. He wasn't disguising his conflicted feelings as well as he'd thought. He rounded the table so that he could better see her face and took one of her hands in his.

"Since the moment I saw you walk onto that stage last night, something about you captivated me. I don't usually take baths or sleep with my subs. You—and what you're making me feel—are what's confusing, Scarlett. I'm in unexplored territory here."

He watched Scarlett's emotions run across her face as he spoke, a barely audible, "Oh," coming from her lips.

He dropped her hand, moved back to the end of the table and picked up another silk strap. He grabbed both her thighs and yanked her down the table until her ass rested at the edge, her knees bent. Taking the silk, he began weaving it between the front and back of her leg, so that it remained bent and couldn't be straightened. His movements were quick and succinct, though jerky with suppressed anger.

"Yes, 'Oh.' So, I'm going to do what I know how to do, and that's fuck you." He finished tying the silk on the first leg and began weaving another restraint around the second.

Surprised that Scarlett was remaining quiet for once, he hoped he hadn't scared her with his confession, but there was also a piece of him that wondered what she was feeling. *Am I the only one who thinks this feels different?* Drew completed the tie and stood directly in front of her spread legs. He ran his hands slowly up each inner thigh until they met at the juncture of her legs. Using both thumbs, he grazed back and forth over her clit, shocked to find that she was already soaking wet. He moaned as his cock got even stiffer.

"You're so wet already. Aren't you even a little bit afraid?"

Her pink tongue darted out, running over her lips, wetting them. "Yes, but I'm excited too."

He shook his head and chuckled. "What am I going to do with you, my little kitten? So curious, so ready to play." He continued to stroke her with only his thumbs, spreading her juices over her entire core, then stopped.

Keeping his eyes on her, he walked slowly around the table and slid one thumb into his mouth, sucking hard. As he sucked, his eyes closed, the taste like a bite of the most delectable dessert. Coming up beside her, he opened his eyes, placed his other thumb against her mouth and pushed. Scarlett sucked hard, pulling his finger all the way into her mouth, moaning as her tongue swirled around it.

His knees grew weak at the sight of her sucking his thumb before he pulled it out of her mouth, bent down and claimed her mouth with his own. He might explode at her luscious taste.

Pulling away from the kiss before he could get carried away, Drew straightened and walked back to the cabinet. He was back in seconds with more silk ties in hand. Scarlett was breathing heavily and her eyes were sparkling with excitement.

"Raise your hands above your head and cross your arms in an X."

She did as he requested, her chest pushing forward, exposing her body further to him, her eyes following his movements. She was shaking, though he knew instinctively that it was from anticipation and not trepidation. He took one wrist and then the other, silently lacing the silk around each in an intricate pattern before securing the binding to a ring.

He stepped back and let his eyes rove over her entire body. "Do you know how unbelievably sexy you look, open and waiting for me?"

"Sir, I'm here to please you."

He let out a huff of laughter in response. "Oh yes! See how the kitten behaves under its mother's paw?"

He traced a finger around one already-taut nipple. "Since you very much wanted my attention on your extremely lovely ass earlier, I think it only fair that I comply now."

Her head snapped up off the table, and for the first time since her arrival, he saw a glint of fear in her eyes.

"Oh, yes, I see I have your full attention now."

He pinched her nipple hard, then bent quickly to take it in his mouth and suckle even harder. She arched off the table in response, groaning at his intensity. She was pulling at her bindings, her fingers splayed out in an attempt to try and touch him, pleading out her frustration at being stuck. He let go of her nipple and walked back down to the end of the table.

"I know you don't have anal play as a hard limit, but I also know it was listed as a possible soft limit. Has anyone ever taken your ass before?" He began caressing the inside of her thighs just shy of her apex, watching as she tried and failed to writhe away from his touch, her bindings holding her in place.

"No, Sir. Not completely. I tried once, but..." Her face was flushed in apparent embarrassment as her sentence trailed off.

"But what?" he pushed.

Her face lightened, and she quickly clenched her eyes shut before opening them to answer him.

"It hurt. So I— We stopped."

She was embarrassed by her admission. He moved his fingers a little closer to her core, applying a bit more pressure now to try and distract her from feeling that way. Her hips surged forward in a short motion, and her knees opened wider.

"If done properly, there should be very little pain, usually just in the beginning, but then it's quite enjoyable. Some women even begin to prefer it over vaginal sex. I'd like very much to show you how enjoyable it can be."

Her core was glistening with wetness, revealing her obvious arousal, but she confirmed it when she nodded, biting her lip before replying with a soft, "Okay, Sir.

He honestly didn't think he could get any harder, but just hearing Scarlett assent to taking her virgin ass caused his cock to swell and strain against the zipper of his jeans. Needing the relief, he unbuttoned his fly, pulled the zipper down and quickly stripped himself naked. He grabbed his thick shaft at the very base and squeezed hard to try and quell the desire to sink into her right then. When the urge dissipated slightly, he grabbed one of the shorter wooden chairs and placed it at the foot of the table.

He positioned himself between Scarlett's spread legs and didn't bother hiding the hungry look in his eyes. Without saying a word, he leaned over, resting his hands at the base of her neck. His fingers were splayed wide as he caressed her throat, slowly moving down until his hands were on her breasts. Her nipples were already hard and tight, so when his fingers grasped each nipple and tugged roughly, her back lunged off the table, causing her head to fall back and a loud moan of pleasure to escape her mouth.

His groin was against her wet core, and she tried to push herself up against his hard length for some relief. He took a small step back, continuing the trail downward with his hands until they landed just above her swollen lips. Again, she pushed herself forward, seeking some kind of relief, mewling a tortured, "Drew, please . . ."

He leaned down, spread her labia wide and blew softly on her clit. Her hips bucked off the table and her moans of pleasure grew louder. "It's my turn to tease you now, my little kitten."

He blew softly again, but this time followed it up by running his tongue over her pussy and lapping at the juices that were flowing from her. While he continued to lick her from front to back, he used one finger to spread her juices down toward her soft, puckered hole. At the first touch of his finger around her hole, she clenched, but as he continued licking her pussy, she gradually relaxed. Then he pushed his finger in quickly up to his middle knuckle. She clenched tightly again and froze.

He raised his head slightly to comfort her. "It's okay. Just breathe out and feel what I'm doing to the rest of your body. I need to stretch you enough to take me."

She rocked her head back and forth as he drowned her in sensation, groaning out an assent. He used his other hand to rub her clit while giving her some direction. "Scarlett, I'm going to push my finger all the way in. I want you to take a deep breath in, and when you breathe out, push down on my finger as I push in."

She did as he asked, and a second later, a small cry escaped her as his finger pushed all the way in. "Good girl. You okay?"

"Yes, yes. I'm okay. Please don't stop now," she panted.

He bent back down between her legs and sucked hard on her clit as he began to piston his finger slowly in and out of her ass. When she started to move with him, into the motion instead of against it, he used the juices flowing freely from her pussy to slip a second finger into her ass. This time, there was very little resistance from her.

She threw her head back and moaned, then hissed. "It burns."

He stilled. "Do you want me to stop?"

She shook her head and rocked her ass against his hand, pushing his fingers deeper. "It feels good too. Just go slow."

His cock jerked at her concession, and he growled in satisfaction. He took his other hand and squeezed a small amount of lubricant where his fingers were inserted. He continued to move two fingers in and out of her ass; she pushed back against him harder now.

"Drew, please, I'm ready for more."

"Shhh, okay Scarlett. You're almost ready." He sucked in his breath at how easily she was opening up to him and begging for more. He began scissoring his fingers to spread her hole wider. He had intended on only inserting the butt plug for now and taking her ass that night, but he was certain neither of them could wait. He slowly pulled his fingers out and grabbed the lubricant he had left next to her hip. He squeezed a generous portion up into her hole and then more into his hand, rubbing it over his rock-hard cock. She watched him, wide eyes locked on his cock.

"Don't worry, it will fit. I'll go really slow. Just tell me if I'm hurting you too much, and I'll stop."

"Are you sure?" Her eyes were still locked on his cock, which was swollen and hard.

"I'm sure."

He grabbed her hips, pulled her to the very edge of the table and lined his cock up with her ass. He held his cock in one hand and slowly started inserting his length into her ass. His cock was throbbing as it started to slide into her hole. She tensed again and tightened like a vise around the tip. He grabbed the vibrator off the table and, turning it on, rubbed it up against the sensitive lips of her pussy and pressed it to her clit.

Her entire body jerked and tightened hard around him before slowly relaxing. "*Oh! Drew!* What are you doing?"

He pushed into her ass a little deeper and didn't know if he was going to be able to fit his whole cock in before he exploded. "Just feel the vibration on your pussy. It will help you through the pain."

He brushed the vibrator back and forth over her pussy as he continued his slow progression into her ass. It was so fucking tight, squeezing his cock, but he could feel her relax and open up as the vibrator starting bringing her closer to orgasm.

Scarlett was panting and grasping the silk ties binding her wrists as she tried to push her ass harder onto his cock. He took the opportunity to thrust the rest of the way in. She yelled out and he stilled for a moment while her body adjusted to his girth. When he felt her relax again, he slid back about an inch, then back in, and then out again.

She started to move with him as moans of pleasure continued to fall from her lips. He dropped the vibrator on the floor, grasped both of her hips with his hands and began to thrust in and out of her hard and quick, his balls slapping the bottom of her ass. His cock swelled even larger as she pushed her hips to meet his, and he knew he wouldn't last much longer.

They were both coated in sweat, eyes closed, moaning loudly. He released one hip and used his fingers to pinch her clit, causing Scarlett to scream his name, fingers wrapped tightly around silk, body stretched taught, her muscles clenching around his cock so hard that he exploded, spilling his release deep inside her.

He fell forward onto her, pressing his forehead to hers, and just breathed for a minute. When he had caught his breath, he kissed her and whispered, "Wow."

She smiled shyly and closed her eyes in satisfaction, her head rolling to the side. Drew straightened up and slowly slid out of her, feeling her wince as he came free.

"Sorry, did that hurt?"

"A little, but it was worth it." Her cheeks flushed a light pink as her gaze fell away. "It was pretty amazing overall."

He moved to the end of the table and started unfastening all the ties securing her. In minutes, he had her in his arms and was carrying her over to the huge bed. He tenderly placed her down and began rubbing the circulation back into her arms and legs. When he got to her shoulders, he ran his finger over the bite mark he had made the night before. A wave of possessiveness washed over him. He bent down and pressed his lips to the bite before trailing his tongue up her neck to find her mouth and capture it in a kiss. He broke away and looked into her eyes.

"You did incredible. You were incredible." He stood up quickly. "I'll be right back."

He returned with a glass of water, some orange pills and a small bowl. He placed the bowl on the floor next to the bed and handed Scarlett the water and pills. "It's ibuprofen. It will help with some of the residual pain." He pulled a washcloth out of the bowl. At her questioning look, he responded, "Just warm water. I cleaned up in the bathroom, but I wanted to take care of you as well."

As Drew finished washing Scarlett, he watched her. She was flush from the exertion they had both endured. Her eyes were shining brightly and were framed by blonde wisps of hair that had escaped from her ponytail. His heart swelled at her beauty and at the innocence she had just entrusted to him. He leaned down and kissed her, holding her face in his hands as he did. She kissed him back, snaking a hand around his neck and feathering her fingers through his hair.

He slowly pulled away but kept his face close to hers. "Are you sure it was okay for you?"

She closed her eyes, blushing, and nodded. "Yes, very much. It was better than I had ever thought it could be."

He leaned down, kissed her nose and, smiling, caressed her cheek. "I'm glad. But now I'll have to come up with another form of punishment the next time you tease me."

She laughed and rolled her eyes. "Well, if it's as good as this punishment, I'll have to make sure I tease you sooner rather than later."

He sat up and shook his head. "You really are a naughty little kitten."

She grinned contentedly. "If I could purr right now, I would."

"Do you want to lie here for a bit or would you like to go back upstairs?"

"Do you mind if we just lay here for a little bit?"

He lay down, pulled her up against him and wrapped his arms around her.

A few hours later, Hannah jerked awake and sat up, forgetting where she was for a moment. Then she saw the St. Andrew's Cross hanging on the wall across the room. *Nothing like a cold dose of reality to wake you up.* She looked down to see Drew on his back, sleeping soundly next to her. God he was beautiful. He really did take her breath away. In more ways than one, apparently. At that thought, her hand flew to her mouth as it formed an O in disbelief. She had just had some of the most amazing sex of her life with this man. And she was the one getting paid. It really didn't seem fair, but there it was.

Domme Maria had warned all the trainees repeatedly that the Doms bought them to serve one purpose: the Dom's pleasure. The subs were to please their Masters at any cost, no matter the pain, pride, or lack of compassion from the Dom. She didn't know if it was the norm, but she seemed to be getting just as much pleasure from this experience as Drew. At least, he *seemed* to be getting pleasure from this. But even more than that, he genuinely seemed to want to please her and make her happy as well.

As she watched him sleep, she ran her fingers over his chest and wondered again why a man this beautiful, this rich, needed to buy a woman for the weekend. Perhaps it was just easier for him? But he seemed like such a kind man. One who would willingly give his heart to the right person. Maybe his heart had been broken one too many times. She sighed and pulled her hand away.

"Don't stop," he mumbled sleepily. "That feels nice."

She put her hand back and continued to caress his chest. "I'm sorry if I woke you."

"It's okay. Much nicer way to wake up than my usual alarm

clock or my assistant calling me at some ungodly hour."

She sat up on her knees and stretched, her hands over her head. She belatedly realized what the pose had done to her breasts when Drew's gaze fell directly on her chest. She lay back down on the bed and, putting her arms around his neck, drew his head to where his gaze had been. Without a word, he pulled a nipple into his mouth and sucked. Her head rolled back on her shoulders as a soft moan escaped from her.

She wrapped her legs around his waist, pulling him flush against her. Their mouths found each other and joined in a slow, sensual tangle of tongues and moans. Her fingers weaved through his hair as his tongue trailed slowly from her mouth to her ear and then down her neck, where he sucked. Soft whimpers of desire left her lips as he lazily trailed his tongue down to her breasts, laving each nipple into hard points before continuing south.

She might die from the pleasure his tongue was bringing her. Every nerve in her skin was heightened by his gentle strokes, leaving her mind in a state of bliss and her body beyond aroused. She'd never had a lover be so gentle, so thorough, so completely in tune with her needs and desires.

As his tongue drew closer to her core, she brushed over her nipples, then pinched them, trying to balance the gentleness with some pain. Moaning in desperation, she pleaded, "Drew, I want you in me."

His hands covered hers, encouraging her to pinch her nipples harder. At the same time, he dragged his tongue across her clit, causing her to moan loudly and buck up against his mouth. He continued to slowly lick and suck her core, still pinching at her nipples, her body on fire. When she thought she wouldn't be able to stand another moment, he rose, slid back up over her body and pushed into her while claiming her mouth in a kiss. Her hands grasped him around his back, nails biting deep into his skin as he pushed deeper and deeper.

Her muscles began to tighten as she felt the familiar build toward her climax, when he suddenly stopped. He kissed her softly then and pulled out. She opened her eyes wide in question but then understood as Drew held tightly to her and rolled over so that she now straddled him. Without a word, he guided her soft core back onto his erect cock.

She started to rock back and forth, her clit sliding against the roughness of him. Her head tilted back and she groaned as he surged harder, her core beginning to tingle again. His arms snaked under hers and pulled her tighter against him, grasping her head in his hands, as he bit out a command through gritted teeth. "Come now, baby! Come with me!"

She could only whimper, "Yes, yes, yes," as she came, meeting each of Drew's thrusts, holding onto him with every ounce of strength she had left. She clenched her eyes tight as her body exploded in a flash of fireworks, sparks flying free, floating away into oblivion.

Drew held Scarlett in his arms, feeling her release and then her complete surrender as he came apart inside of her. He rolled her onto her side, holding her gently, not wanting to separate himself from her yet. As if she could read his mind, she adjusted her body and melted into him, releasing a deep, satisfied breath. He lay there, holding her for several minutes, before sliding himself out of her. He pulled her hand into his and held it against his lips, kissing her knuckles lightly. "Thank you for the best morning I've had in a while."

"I could say the same to you," she whispered, squeezing his hand in return.

His heart thundered in his chest as he realized he may have just wandered into dangerous territory. He was supposed to be fucking away his worries this weekend, but what he'd just done with Scarlett went beyond fucking for him. Every time he tried to draw a line with her, he seemed to cross it. And what was worse was that this was her first time; she likely didn't realize that this wasn't normal behavior from him or any Dom.

Her stomach grumbled as she lay flush against him, and then she giggled.

"Hungry?"

"I won't even try to deny it this time!"

He dropped her hand and sat up, looking down at her reclining form, smiling. "That's what good sex will do to you."

He stood and extended his hand to help her from the bed. As they walked to the stairs, he gathered their clothing and carried it up with them.

Once they were back in the main house, he stopped at the phone in the entryway. "What would you like to eat? I think I'll just call in the chef to make us something for lunch."

Scarlett tilted her head in thought. "Would you think I'm crazy if I told you that a grilled cheese and tomato soup sound heavenly to me right now?"

He smiled broadly. "That actually sounds delicious. I can't remember the last time I had a grilled cheese. I'm sure it was probably years ago and made by my mother."

"It's a staple at my house. We love them." Scarlett smiled back at him.

His brow furrowed for a moment, causing Scarlett a moment of pause. "Are you okay?"

He recovered quickly and smiled. "Yes. I'm fine. You go ahead and shower. I'll call the kitchen and order for us, then shower in the spare to give you a bit of space."

She bowed slightly, grinning. "Why, thank you, kind Sir. Any requests on attire?"

"Surprise me." He watched as Scarlett's naked ass disappeared into the bedroom. He tilted his head. *Who the hell was "we"?*

Chapter Six

"Dammit, Scott, you knew I was off-limits this weekend! Is it impossible for you to handle this one thing?"

Drew paced the length of the kitchen, feet landing hard with each step, as Scarlett silently sat on one of the stools at the bar where two covered trays waited. Jesus, she was wearing navy blue silk—the same color he'd tied her up in. He gave her an apologetic look and then held up a finger to indicate he would be a moment. Scott was clamoring on about a complication with one of the hotels being built. He could really care less at this point but knew his father would and knew it had to be dealt with.

"Fine, fine. Give me fifteen minutes and I'll call you back. I need to deal with something else right now." He clicked end on the phone screen and raked his hands through his hair in frustration before turning back to Scarlett.

"Time to deal with me now?" she quipped and then instantly regretted it as his expression morphed from frustration to anger. That was exactly something his ex-wife would have said to him, and the last thing he wanted to hear from Scarlett.

"Scarlett, not now." He walked over to the bar, removing the cover from both trays and sitting down beside her.

"Let's eat. I only have fifteen minutes."

He pushed one of the trays closer to her and noticed her head was down, an apologetic look on her face. She turned her face toward him timidly. "I'm sorry. It wasn't my place to speak to you that way."

He shook his head, frustrated at having to explain himself, and placed his spoon down on the counter. "No, I'm sorry. Everyone knows I'm off-limits this weekend, but something came up that can't wait, and I need to deal with it."

He brushed a lock of hair away from her face, hooking it behind her ear. He took his finger and, placing it under her chin, lifted her head up. "Look at me, Scarlett."

She raised her eyes, meeting his intent stare.

"My job demands a lot from me." He sighed, wondering how much he should share with her before continuing. "I was married once. She left me because she said my job always came first. I'm trying really hard to separate my personal time from my business, but there are always situations that can't be avoided."

He dropped his hand, placing it back on the counter but continued to look her in the eye.

She was looking at him with surprise on her face. "Drew, I'm sorry. I didn't realize. I mean, I didn't mean to infer—"

He put his hand up to interrupt her. "Stop. How could you? You just hit a nerve. You're actually the first person in a long time to make me want to forget about my job. No more apologies. Let's just eat lunch."

He leaned forward and brushed his lips against hers, lightly at first but then becoming more intense as both of her hands came up to his face and pulled him in closer. He pulled away after a moment, breaking the kiss with a few smaller ones, and then leaned back.

"I'm really sorry, Drew."

He nodded and then turned back to their lunches.

"We should eat before this gets any colder."

He dipped a corner of his sandwich into his soup and took a generous bite, groaning loudly. "I forgot how amazing these are!"

She laughed and took a bite of her sandwich. "See? I told you!"

When they had both finished their soups and sandwiches, Scarlett got up to put the dirty dishes in the sink. He got up and followed behind her, startling her when she turned around.

"What are you doing?"

Instead of responding, he stepped forward, forcing her to take a step back and bump up against the sink. He placed both hands beside her on the counter, leaned down and whispered into her ear, "I love you in that color. I can't wait to wrap you up in it again."

He ran his nose down her cheek until his lips met hers in a sensuous kiss. She wrapped her arms around his neck, clutching his hair in her fingers, deepening the kiss. He groaned loudly and then pulled apart from her.

"Every time I'm in this kitchen, I want to throw you up on this counter and have my way with you."

"So do it. I'm not stopping you." She reached out to pull him back to her, but he put his hands up and walked backward, smiling.

"I've never hated my job more than I do right now, but I have to go make these calls or I'm afraid I'll be pulled away even longer. "

She pushed her lower lip out, pouting, and ran her hands seductively up her body, over her breasts, then leaned back into the counter. "Okay, well, I'll be ready whenever you are."

He raised his eyebrows. "Are you teasing me again, naughty little kitten?"

She shook her head. "Nope. Just making you a promise."

He clucked his tongue as he turned and walked away. "Oh, I'm going to hold you to that promise, beautiful."

Hannah couldn't help the huge smile that spread across her face as Drew walked away. He wanted her. He really wanted her. She was doing this submissive thing right. It was going better than she had thought it would. Still smiling, she walked into the bedroom. She decided she would go outside and spend some time by the pool. The sun was out and maybe she could catch some extended summer sun. She opened the wardrobe to look for a bathing suit. She found a simple black bikini and pulled it on. The top had ample coverage, but when she turned around and looked in the mirror, more of her ass was showing than was covered. *Hmm, not half bad*, she thought, deciding to keep it on.

She walked into the living room and opened the French doors that led out to the pool. One of the advantages to staying in a bungalow was that each one had its very own private pool and hot tub. The back yard was completely surrounded by an eight-foot oak fence but was beautifully landscaped with flowers and bushes to create an almost tropical feel. After grabbing some sunscreen and a towel from a cabinet against the house, she made her way over to one of the lounge chairs.

It was a gorgeous day without a cloud in the sky. If only she'd thought to bring her phone out so she could listen to some music, but she was too comfortable to get up and go back in the house. Instead, her head filled with thoughts of Drew and the time they had spent together so far. As this was her first auction experience—well, her first submissive experience, if she was being honest—she had no idea if the way Drew was being with her was expected.

Domme Maria had given the impression that her time as a submissive would be much more taxing in nature. But thus far, Drew had demanded very little of her, and this seemed more like a weekend spent with a lover than a Dominant. The sexual chemistry between them was instant and electric, and in no way was she "performing." She was truly enjoying his company and had to admit the sex was amazing. She wasn't going to fool herself into thinking all outcomes with a Dominant would be this easy or natural. She had gotten lucky.

After a half hour in the hot sun, she was in danger of melting if she didn't get into the pool. She dove in gracefully and swam a few laps before stopping in the shallow end. She used the stairs to climb out of the pool and walk back to her chair. She could see Drew pacing in the living room, talking to someone on his phone. It certainly didn't seem like he was going to be done anytime soon.

Before lying back down, she looked around nervously and wondered if she could get away with sunning topless. The perimeter fence seemed to completely obscure any possibility of anyone outside the yard from seeing her. Safe enough then. She untied her top, dropping it next to her chair before lying on her stomach and stretching her hands overhead. She lay there, listening to the gentle breeze and birds chirping, and slowly drifted to sleep.

Hannah felt something tug on her wrists and slowly opened her eyes. She was met with Drew's smoldering glare as he kneeled down at the head of her chair. She glanced at her hands and was startled to see that they'd been bound to the top slat of the chair with her bikini top.

"Good afternoon, sleeping beauty," Drew said before rising to his full height.

She was still lying on her stomach and had to lean her head all the way back to keep her eyes on his. She looked down at her hands quickly, tugging, and then back up at him. "What are you doing?"

"The question is what were *you* doing?" He walked toward the foot of the chair. She tried to follow him with her eyes but found it difficult due to her bindings.

"I-I-I'm not sure what you mean. I've just been lying by the pool."

Instead of answering, he grasped the waist of her bathing suit on each side of her hips and pulled it down and off her. His hand traced back up her leg and then rested on her ass. He started rubbing her cheeks in a slow, circular motion. He finally spoke, and it wasn't gentle.

"Don't you mean you've just been lying by this pool without your top on? Where anyone could have entered and seen you?"

She was surprised he was so angry. "But, Sir, there is a fence. It seemed safe to me."

Drew scoffed in disagreement. "You think it's safe? I decide what's safe for you. And where it's safe for you. And most of all, I decide when you take your clothes off."

She was trying to form another response when his hand stopped caressing her ass and suddenly came down in a hard smack. She yelped in surprise, stopping any reply that had been on her lips.

His hand rose again, and she prepared herself for another smack. She wasn't disappointed. This one was harder than the last. She felt him sit and slide her legs up and over his lap.

"Do you know why I'm spanking you, Scarlett?" His voice was harsh, his breathing heavy. He was excited by this. And that excited her.

"Yes, Sir. Only you are allowed to see me this way," she replied huskily, already anticipating the next smack against her ass.

"That's right. And to make sure you remember, you'll get ten smacks. I want you counting out loud."

He brought his hand up and down again ten more times, each time a little harder than the last, waiting for her to count between each one. After the tenth smack, he rubbed her ass lightly, his breathing heavy. His lips kissed one side of her buttocks, and then his fingers rubbed over her pussy. She was soaking wet, and he sucked in a breath when he felt it.

Then he chuckled, still gliding his fingers over her. "You liked that?"

There was no way she could say otherwise. Her core was pulsating from the vibrations of his spanking and she wanted nothing more than to climax. "Yes."

As if he could read her mind, he stuck two fingers inside her and started pumping them back and forth. She opened her legs wider, pushing herself back into his hand as she whimpered in ecstasy.

He grabbed onto her hip with his other hand, steadying her. "You want me deeper, Scarlett?"

"Oh god," she breathed out, "please, Drew, yes."

Drew could feel his cock getting hard but pushed down his desire. He pushed his fingers deeper into Scarlett, and as her muscles started to clench, he pulled out and slid her off his lap, standing up. Her head spun around to look at him, shock on her face.

"What are you doing? Why did you stop?"

He kneeled down beside her so that his face was even with hers.

Then he slowly inserted the two fingers that had just been inside Scarlett into his mouth and sucked.

"Mmm, you taste so good." He felt wicked as she stared at him, mouth open, eyes wide in disbelief. "Don't take your clothes off again where someone could see you."

He reached up then and quickly untied the bikini top, rubbing her arms to bring circulation back into them.

"You are evil, Drew. Pure and simple." She sat up, glaring at him.

"Believe me, this hurts me almost as much as you." He looked down at the prominent bulge in his jeans.

"I can help you with that if you want," she offered suggestively.

"Maybe later. I think my cock needs a break, even if it doesn't realize it."

He lay down behind her on the lounge chair and pulled her back to his front, wrapping his arms around her. He nuzzled her hair, inhaling deeply, savoring the smell of the oil and sun on her, but also the light floral scent that always seemed to be on her skin.

"You smell good," he rumbled into her ear and pulled her in closer. Hannah smiled but didn't reply. She was enjoying being in his embrace and the simplicity of the moment. She ran her fingers up and down the length of his arm, grazing the downy hair that covered it. When she touched his hand, he pulled her fingers into his, entwining them, and held her there. They stayed like that for a long time before Drew finally kissed her head, released her and sat up.

She sat up as well and faced him. He stroked her cheek lovingly and then leaned forward, capturing her lips in a gentle kiss. He pulled slowly away, never breaking eye contact with her. She was starting to feel nervous, as this seemed entirely too intimate for what her purpose was supposed to be. She broke his gaze by looking down at her hands and cleared her throat, unsure of what to do next. Luckily, he broke the silence.

"I have a surprise for you."

She raised her head in apprehension, not sure if she could take any more surprises. "Really? Good or bad?"

Drew laughed. "It's a good one. I think."

He stood up, pulling her with him. He grabbed the towel on the chair and wrapped it around her, pulling her close. He leaned down and whispered into her ear, "Do you want to go to a party?"

She looked up at him and smiled. "What kind of party?"

"The kind where you get to dress up like a princess."

"Then yes!" She jumped up and down in place like a little child, unable to contain her glee.

"Good. Because I have a whole team of people inside, at your beck and call, to help you get ready."

She stopped jumping up and down and looked at Drew, eyebrows drawn up, her hand covering her mouth. "Oh my god, Drew. Were they inside while you were spanking me?"

His reply was casual and dismissive. "Yes, but believe me, it's nothing they haven't seen or heard before."

Her face turned a bright crimson. "I have to go in there now knowing that they probably either saw or heard everything you just did to me?" She covered her face with her hands, groaning, "I'm so embarrassed."

Drew grasped her roughly around the neck, pulling her face close to his, and practically growled, "Are you saying you're embarrassed to be with me? Because I'm pretty sure any one of the people in the next room would be more than happy to take your place."

She balked at his tone and the callousness of his statement. She couldn't keep up with his hot and cold behavior. Less than ten minutes ago, he'd been holding her hand in an act of surprising intimacy, and now he was suddenly reminding her she was simply a paid servant. She fell back into submissive mode. "No, Sir. I'm only embarrassed that someone may have been watching us."

Drew pulled her in closer and whispered in her ear, "I don't care who is watching. As long as I'm the one that's with you." He kissed her roughly and let go of her neck.

He started walking away toward the house. "Come. Let's go meet your entourage." And just like that, any anger he expressed was gone.

Am I a dog now? Cause that's what that last command felt like. Hannah shook her head in confusion but quickly followed so she wouldn't provoke another outburst of anger.

Chapter Seven

Walking into the house, Hannah hugged the towel tightly to her chest to ensure it didn't slip and reveal any more surprises to the staff waiting inside. Drew stopped at the opened door, waiting for her to pass through. Surprisingly, there was no one in sight.

"Where are they?" she asked quietly as she stepped further into the living room.

Drew closed the door behind her and once again pulled her close before speaking. "Do you really think I would risk anyone else seeing you naked?"

She wasn't sure how to reply, so she remained quiet, her eyes on his feet. He placed his finger under her chin, lifting it. "I had the staff set up and wait for you in the master suite. I don't want to share you with anyone, Scarlett. You are mine and only mine. Understood?"

"At least until tomorrow," she replied quietly, knowing she might just be adding fuel to a simmering fire.

As if burned, he dropped his hand suddenly and took a step back. He took a deep breath as he looked up at the ceiling, eyes closed. He blew the breath back out slowly and, returning his gaze to her, nodded.

"Well, until tomorrow then." He turned quickly away from her and started walking to the bedroom. "Come."

She wanted to scream in frustration over the mixed signals he was sending her but instead just stayed quiet and did as he commanded. When she came around the corner to the doorway of the bedroom, she could hear chatter that immediately stopped when they saw Drew. He stopped just beyond the entrance to the room and motioned for her to enter before addressing the staff.

"You have two hours." And then he turned and walked away. She watched him leave, surprised at the way he'd addressed them and at the lack of any to her. She sighed and then turned her head back to the staff.

"Oh my god! Just look at you!" She finally took in the staff Drew had left her with. A young Asian man, dressed in shiny black pants and an even shinier silver button-down shirt, came forward and circled her, arms waving above his head as he went. "Drew said you were beautiful, but this is just too much!

"Karla! Laura! Are you seeing this?" he exclaimed loudly to the two other women in the room.

A small, wavy-haired brunette took one of Hannah's hands—which were still clutching her towel—and led her further into the room. "Yes, Marco. We see her. But please, stop! You're scaring the poor thing! Just look at her!"

Turning to the other woman in the room, the brunette continued, "Karla, you are so lucky! Look at all this beautiful hair you get to work with!"

Karla, now that Hannah knew what her name was, had long blonde hair, similar to her own, running like strands of silk down her entire back. Jealous did not even begin to describe the envy Hannah felt at its beauty. The woman looked a bit bored with Marco and the brunette's whole excited routine and just nodded her head before drawling, "Yes, well, we only have two hours, so we better get to work."

"Oh, Karla, you're such a little grouch!" Marco shot an exasperated look at the blonde and then followed behind Hannah into the large attached dressing room.

"First things first!" Marco continued in a rush. "We have to show you your dress and make sure it fits." Hannah gasped at the creation hanging from the center of the room.

"Oh my god," she whispered. "Is that for me?"

Marco slapped her playfully on the arm and replied gleefully, "Of course it's for you! Do you love it?"

"It's absolutely gorgeous." She padded closer in excitement. In the front, the dress was held up by a single strap embroidered with diamonds that wound up and over the shoulder. More diamonds spilled down the left side waist and wrapped around to join four straps that angled diagonally across the back, joining the shoulder strap. The sheer silk fabric was pitch black starting at the shoulder but spilled down in an ombré effect, turning to a deep, royal blue at the floor-length hem of the full skirt. Under the top layer of silk, a fitted, black satin sheath was attached.

Of course he would choose royal blue. It seemed to be his color of choice. She ran her hand over the luxurious fabric and marveled at its softness. She turned to the three others in the room, who had been standing quietly while she admired the dress. "I feel like freaking Cinderella!"

She started jumping up and down, clapping her hands in excitement. Marco rushed over, grasping both of her hands in his. "Well then, let's try it on, Cinderella, and see if it fits!"

"Yes, please!" She could not contain her astonishment at wearing this splendor of a dress and smiled from ear to ear as Marco removed it from the hanger so she could try it on.

"Drop that towel, darling. The dress isn't going to fit over it."

She looked down at the towel and then up at Marco, the spanking she had just endured fresh in her mind and still stinging her buttocks. "Oh, I don't think I had better do that in front of you. I don't think Drew would like that."

Marco waved one of his hands in disagreement. "Listen, darling, I'm about as interested in seeing you naked as I would be my grandmother. You just don't have what I'm looking for. Get my drift?"

"Oh!" She caught his meaning quickly and blushed at his candor. So, without further ado, she dropped the towel and let Marco help her into the dress.

After zipping up the side, he strolled around her, hmming and umming under his breath while shifting some of the fabric, placing a few pins strategically to fit the dress on her before finally exclaiming, "It's almost perfect. You would think I had made this dress for you!"

She beamed at him. "It feels comfortable. Do you want me to walk around at all? It seems a bit long."

"That's because you don't have the shoes on yet, darling! But yes, do a little walk around for me please so I can see it move on you."

She paraded back and forth across the dressing room, twirling at each turn, watching as the bottom of the skirt swished out each time.

"Okay, you're good. Let's get you out of it now. I just have to make a few little adjustments." Marco helped her unzip the dress and step out of it. She quickly grabbed the towel lying on the floor and wrapped it around her.

"Not so quick!" Laura—the curly-haired brunette—was snapping orders at her now. "You need to shower and wash your hair. But be quick please, we have so little time."

"Okay, I'll be extra quick." Hannah scurried out of the dressing room and made her way to the shower as ordered.

Fifteen minutes later, she was covered in her robe and sitting at the dressing table as Karla brushed her hair and Laura removed her current polish from her finger and toenails. "Mr. Sapphire wants your hair up, but I think we need to add a little framing around your face, so I will blow your front out a bit straighter and curl your hair in the back, okay?"

"Who's Mr. Sapphire?" Hannah asked curiously. Both girls stopped what they were doing and looked at her strangely.

Laura replied in a shocked tone, "Andrew Sapphire. You know, the gorgeous one who brought you in here?"

"Of course!" She laughed nervously, trying to cover up her mistake. "I'm so used to calling him Drew that I totally spaced out!"

Both girls looked at her like she had two heads and resumed their work.

His name is Andrew Sapphire? How could I have fucked someone four—or was it five?—times in the last twenty-four hours and not known his full name? But then, I guess he doesn't know my real name either. And now all the blue makes sense . . . Hannah twisted her hands together as the reality of her situation hit her. She was so caught up in this moment and the way he had been making her feel that she'd forgotten that this was just a job. She needed to get herself back in line, and quickly, before her heart completely took over.

The next hour and a half flew by as Karla curled and primped and pinned her hair into the most amazing hairstyle she had ever worn. The stylist had created large, curly waves, then swept them to the side of her head in a large bun and pinned them up loosely so that a few locks of hair dangled down. The front was swept over to the same side and pulled into a side bun, again with a few longer, curled strands left out to frame her face.

Her makeup was heavier than she normally wore, but it still looked minimal on her, only enhancing her features. Laura had outlined Hannah's upper lid in a popular cat-eye style and then softened it with a darker blue shadow, highlighted by a swipe of silver. Soft, pink cheeks and lips brought it all together. Laura had also discreetly applied some cover-up over the fading bite mark on her shoulder without so much as a word about it. Hannah's fingers and toes were now covered with a silver nail polish that she normally would have thought a bit too bold but matched perfectly the diamonds embroidered on her dress.

Before Marco would allow her to step into the dress, Laura and Karla worked to strap on the most amazing shoes that had ever been on her feet. The base of each shoe was silver, elevated by a thin, four-inch stiletto heel. A single, inch-wide silver strap crossed the top of the shoe, embroidered with the same diamonds on the dress. The back of the shoe connected to another inch-wide silver strap, similarly embroidered, that wrapped around her ankle and tied in the back with a silver ribbon. It appeared as though she was wearing diamond cuffs on her ankles. Had Cinderella felt this wondrous about the shoes she'd worn to the ball?

Finally, Marco allowed her to step into the now-altered dress, and zipped her up. Her personal beauty team of three all stepped back and simply gazed at her without saying a word. "What?" Hannah exclaimed. "You're all making me nervous!"

Marco, as usual, was the first to speak. "Oh, darling, it's just that you are so unbelievably stunning. Just a vision." Laura nodded in agreement, eyes wide in wonder. Karla just nodded, a satisfied, if not smug, smile on her lips.

"Are you sure?" Hannah asked, unconvinced, working her hands nervously over the skirt of the dress.

"I'm sure." Drew's rich voice sounded from behind, and she spun around, almost losing her balance on her four-inch stilettos.

"Out. Now." Drew's gaze was fixed on her, but he made it clear that Marco and the ladies were done.

Marco clapped his hands. "Come, girls, grab your things! It's time to go."

Like little mice, they quickly gathered their tools and scurried out of the room. As Marco walked by, he pecked Hannah on the cheek and beamed with pride. The front door slammed behind them as they left.

Drew was still staring at her, having not moved a step or spoken another word. He was wearing a traditional tuxedo, but instead of a bow tie, he wore a dark, royal-blue silk tie in a Windsor knot.

"Do I look okay, Sir?"

He took a step forward and then circled around her, examining her from every angle. "Something is missing."

"Is there? I think Marco did everything you requested." She inhaled deeply, savoring the scent Drew left in his wake. It was crisp and light, but carried with it a subtle cedar-and-musk undertone. It immediately aroused her senses and made her want to run her hand up his neck so that she could bring him closer and nuzzle him.

He walked over to a drawer on the far side of the closet and opened it. He reached inside and pulled out two teal suede boxes. And not just any blue—they were Tiffany blue. She practically swooned just seeing the boxes.

"That's because this is something only I can do." He beckoned for her to follow him to the full-length mirror against the opposite wall of the dressing room. He set the boxes down on a table and turned toward her.

"Do you know what a submissive collar is?" he asked her quietly, his hand still lying over the boxes on the table.

"Yes, Sir." When a Dom and a sub entered into an exclusive relationship, one that involved a commitment almost as strong as a marriage, the sub was very often collared, demonstrating ownership to everyone else. "But . . ."

"But what, Scarlett?" He still spoke quietly.

"But I am only yours for another day. You couldn't possible want to collar me." Her hand rose involuntarily to her neck, her fingers running around its base absently.

"Oh, but that's where you're wrong. I very much want to collar you. Even if it is just for another twenty-four hours." He moved behind her, resting his hands on either side of her shoulders.

"Look at yourself. Can you see what I see?"

She looked at her reflection in the mirror. She did look beautiful. More so than she had been before. But it was the clothes, the hair, and the makeup. This wasn't really her. "I suppose I see myself, but made up to be what you want me to be."

He shook his head in disagreement. "Oh, Scarlett, you are exactly who you should be, and that is just you. Yes, you're beautiful, but it's your grace, your charm and your wit that will grab anyone's attention. I intend to make sure everyone knows you belong to me, and only me."

With that, he reached down and opened the larger of the two boxes sitting on the table. She gasped at what lay inside. It was the most exquisite diamond necklace she had ever seen. Eight rows of diamonds circled in a lace-like collar.

"Do you like it?" He looked at her in the mirror as he pulled it out of the box and unclasped it.

"Like it? Drew, it's amazing." She raised her hand to stop him from putting it on. "Are you sure?"

"About collaring you?"

She looked at him, trying to assess if this was a trivial moment for him, but as always, his face remained neutral.

He turned her around, raising the intensity of the moment, and looked in her eyes while he answered. "I'm sure. Are you?"

"I-I don't know." She tilted her head. "I know I shouldn't ask this, but I'm just going to anyway. Is this something you do to all your submissives?"

His eyes narrowed in thought at her question before he broke his gaze and turned her back toward the mirror. His hands brought the choker around the front of her, and then his fingers trailed over the diamonds before fastening it.

She looked up, meeting his eyes in the mirror, and she could see desire coursing through them, darker than she'd ever them before.

"No. I've never put a collar on someone before."

Her heart hammered in her chest at what this implied. Even though some of his behavior toward her had seemed too intimate, this act definitely confirmed he was feeling more for her than he should.

He chuckled low as he opened the other box. "Don't worry, Scarlett, it's just for the weekend. I promise I'll take it off later."

Although the comment was meant to offer her some relief, it didn't. She tried to push back her confusion and questions until a later time. She didn't want to spoil this moment, whatever it was. Even though she didn't want to admit it to herself, deep down, she was secretly thrilled that he was claiming her. She liked Drew, more than she probably should, and wanted to stay in this fairy-tale bubble for a little while longer before having to think about the real world again.

"There's more?" she spluttered, watching as he opened the second box. It was overwhelming.

"Only one more thing." Out of the second box, which was smaller and squarer in shape, he pulled a matching cuff and secured it around her left wrist.

"Now you're complete." He looked at her again in the mirror, eyes smoldering. "You look absolutely ravishing. There should be no doubt in anyone's mind who you belong to."

"I'm yours," she whispered, not breaking his gaze in the mirror.

He grasped her chin, tilting her mouth back to his, and kissed her fiercely and quickly. "Fuck yes. Hearing you say that makes me so hard."

She was practically panting and really didn't care anymore about going to some ball. She reached her hand back to feel his erection, rubbing it through the material of his pants. He chuckled and grabbed her wrist, stopping her motions.

"As much as I'd like to ravish you right here, we need to go so we won't be late." He kissed her softly on her forehead and shifted his grip from around her wrist to her hand instead. He led her out of the dressing room and through the bedroom.

"One second please; I just need to grab my clutch." Earlier, Marco had given her a small, black satin clutch with just a few scattered diamond stones embroidered on the edging. Laura had given her an extra lipstick and powder compact for touch-ups throughout the night. Those were the only items in the clutch.

"You shouldn't need a thing. I'll be taking care of everything."

"It's just lipstick and powder. You know, for touch-ups and such." She smiled at him.

"Very good." He extended his arm to her, which she took, and led her out of the house to a waiting car.

"Are we driving?" she inquired as he helped her into the front seat of the sleek black car.

"Yes. I'm driving." He shut the door before she could ask any more questions, walked around to the driver's side and seated himself in the car. He started it, backing out of the driveway, and then slowly proceeded through the compound. When he got to the large wrought-iron gates, he slowed to a stop and rolled down the window.

The guard seemed to recognize him immediately. "Oh hello, Mr. Sapphire." He tipped his hat at him before walking to a switch and activating it, allowing the gates to swing open wide. "You're clear to leave."

"Thank you, Jones." Drew nodded as he rolled up the window and then zipped through the gates and out of the compound.

Chapter Eight

Drew pulled onto the main road, shifting the car into a higher gear, and accelerated, scenery starting to slide quickly past the windows of the car.

"Drew, why are we leaving the estate?" Scarlett asked. "I didn't think we were allowed off the grounds."

"Don't worry. I got permission from Domme Maria." He looked over at her with a mischievous grin on his face. "You don't think I would break the rules do you?"

"Did it occur to you to ask *me* if I wanted to be taken off of the grounds?"

He was surprised by the indignant tone in her voice and glanced over to see if he could read her face. If anything, he was taken aback that she would be angry.

"Why are you upset about us leaving the estate? You do know that I would never do anything to harm you, correct?"

She shook her head, responding, "I'm upset that you didn't think to ask me. It's great that you asked Domme Maria, but this should have been my choice."

Drew swerved the car over to the side of the road, putting it into park. "Scarlett, I'll ask you again: do you really think I would do anything to hurt you? Take you somewhere that would bring you harm? Have I treated you so badly over the last two days?"

She took his hands in hers, squeezing them briefly. "Of course I don't think you would hurt me. I would have never let you do what you did to me today if I didn't trust you."

"Then what is it?" Anger still edged his response.

"It should have been my choice to leave the grounds. Not something you should have assumed I would want to do. I don't know where we are going. How do I explain you if I run into someone I know?"

He stared at her blankly. It hadn't really occurred to him to ask her, or that she might know someone. That was an assumption he shouldn't have made. Especially given the fact that he knew nothing about her. He found himself in new territory once again; he actually felt remorse. He moved his hands over hers now, holding them lightly. The bracelet looked stunning on her wrist.

"I apologize then. I assumed when I told you we'd be going to a party that you understood it wasn't on the estate. I should have explained further. Would you still like to go?"

"May I ask where we are going first?" Scarlett spoke quietly from her side of the car.

"It's a charity ball. In the city. Normally, I wouldn't have attempted to attend something of this nature on a weekend like this, but the cause is very dear to my heart."

"Then yes, I'd like to go with you to the ball." She was quiet for a moment and then giggled, taking her hand from his, covering her mouth as her cheeks flushed pink. "I feel like I just got asked to the prom!"

He turned back in his seat, smiling broadly, relief washing over him that she no longer seemed angry, and pulled the car back out onto the road to continue their journey. "We can pretend if you want. I never went to my prom."

"What?" Her voice held a note of surprise. "How is that possible? You're like perfect prom-king material."

He scoffed before responding, "My father only saw me as the heir to his business, so going to dances and parties was beneath my station. He made sure I only had time for schoolwork, and if I wasn't doing that, I was working for him."

"That's pretty sad."

He shrugged. "It is what it is. It wasn't all bad. I traveled all over the world. Believe me, I had my share of fun when my father wasn't watching."

"You said the charity was close to your heart? Can I ask what the ball is for?"

Drew looked over at her, eyebrow raised, not immune to her attempt at moving the subject away from his father. He smiled inwardly at her ability to recognize a difficult topic for him.

"It's a charity for disabled veterans and their families. Do you know how many vets come back from the Middle East and get no help at all? It's a shame. Or even worse, soldiers are killed and not enough is done to support any family they leave behind."

Hannah jolted in surprise. *What a small world it is.* "Do you know someone who was there?"

Drew took his gaze off the road and looked at her. "Yes."

"I'm sorry. I truly am." *I know more about this than he can possibly imagine.*

"Thank you. I'm lucky, I suppose. My brother came home. Even if it took us a long time to actually get him back."

She sat quietly for a few moments, looking out the window at the trees flying by, lost in her own thoughts. The lights of Manhattan were looming ahead, and she wondered again about the party.

"How will you introduce me tonight? I mean, in case we see someone I know or someone you know."

He let out a little huff of laughter. "Oh, I'm sure we'll see some people I know, and I'm sure they'll be asking about you. I haven't brought anyone to a function with me since my divorce."

"What?" She couldn't contain the shock in her voice. *He hasn't brought anyone else since his divorce? Sweet Jesus, this is getting complicated.*

"Don't worry. Very few people know about my alternate lifestyle. I'll simply tell them you're my date."

"And they'll just accept that?" *Sure they will.*

"Ha. Probably not. But that's all they'll be getting. Are you really worried you'll see people here you know? The tickets were twenty-five hundred a place setting, Scarlett."

Instead of being offended, she just shrugged and raised an eyebrow at him.

"Snobby much? Besides, you just might be surprised."

He raised his eyebrows back at her. "Touché." There was a moment of silence between them before he continued. "Besides, neither one of us has to worry about anyone recognizing us. Want to know why?"

She eyed him curiously. "Why?"

A devilish grin spread across his face. "It's a masquerade ball. We'll have masks on the entire time. We can even make up names for ourselves if we want."

She laughed at that. "My name *is* made up, Drew."

"Ah, yes. I guess that makes it even easier then, doesn't it?" he responded in kind.

"I suppose so," she said. "But that means we have to come up with something for you now, doesn't it?"

"I already thought of the perfect name."

"Oh, I can't wait. Please, tell me how I should address you this evening—besides Master, of course."

He responded in a forced Southern accent, "Why Miss Scarlett, I'm surprised you even have to ask."

She immediately caught the reference. Was he really going to pick the name Rhett? Could he possibly know why she had picked the name Scarlett as her alternate identity? The mounting coincidences left her mind reeling.

Hiding her bewilderment, she simply responded in her best Southern drawl. "Why Mr. Butler, I do declare, this might actually be a fun evening after all!"

They both laughed and finally, the heavy mood that had started their evening seemed to lighten.

"I've never been to a masquerade party before. Have you?"

"Yes, several actually." He glanced at her and winked. "But this is the first one I've actually looked forward to in quite some time. I think perhaps the company helps."

"Why thank you, kind Sir." She blushed as she replied, warmed by the fact that he seemed to want to be with her as much as she wanted to be with him.

"That's actually the reason Domme Maria allowed me to bring you off of the estate this evening. She knew your identity would be safe. Do you feel better about attending now?" he asked quietly.

"It's not that I ever minded going. I just would have liked to be asked. That's all."

"Well, I'm grateful you said yes." He motioned out the window to her. "We're here."

He pulled the car into the long circular drive of a hotel and waited in a line of cars for the valet. As the valet approached, Drew stepped out of the car and grabbed something from the backseat. He took a ticket from the young man, then walked around to her side of the car, opening the door and holding out one hand to assist her.

She rose up gracefully before him. With her heels on, she was much taller than normal and could almost look him in the eyes now. Well, maybe his lips. But that wasn't such a bad view either. Before she could help herself, she leaned forward and pressed a kiss to them.

"I'm sorry we fought in the car," she said as she pulled away from him. "I didn't mean to make you angry."

He smiled back at her, his eyes crinkling. "You do seem to do that a lot, don't you?"

He leaned down and kissed her this time and then whispered in her ear, "But you also seem to have a way of making me forget all about it moments later."

"Here, turn around; I have to put your mask on before we go inside."

"Wait, can I see it first?" she asked eagerly.

"Of course. I forgot you hadn't seen it. Marco had these made for us as well."

He held out a mask for her perusal. It was breathtaking. Black silk had been woven together to create beautiful swirls around the eyeholes, swooping up over the eyes like feathers. The same diamonds that were sewn onto her dress has also been scattered over the mask. The ties were made of delicate black lace woven tightly together to allow them to be tied more easily.

"Oh, Drew, it's lovely. Will you put it on?" She looked up at him adoringly as she handed the mask back to him.

"With pleasure." He carefully placed it on her face, lining up the eyes properly before wrapping the lace straps around her head and tying it in place.

"Is it comfortable?"

"Yes, it feels perfect. Do you need help with yours?" But he was already tying his mask into place. His was a much simpler mask, made of a solid black piece of silk cut into a standard eye-mask shape. The blue of his eyes stood in such contrast to the black of the mask, making him look more handsome than she thought possible.

He held his arm out to her, his terrible Southern accent appearing again. "All right, Miss Scarlett, if you're ready, I'll escort you in."

She settled her arm into the crook of his, leaning into him as they walked. She liked feeling the warmth that always seemed to radiate from him. In moments, they were being ushered into a huge ballroom within the hotel. Its grandeur was something to behold. Large, round tables lined the perimeter of the room. Each table was covered in sapphire-colored tablecloths, and held eight place settings, silverware gleaming and crystal sparkling. The floral centerpieces on each table consisted of beautiful white orchids that scented the entire ballroom. The center of the room was kept clear for a dance floor, and the front of the room held a stage on which an orchestra played. She gazed around at the opulence in wonder and couldn't believe that she was actually attending this event.

The room was quite loud, as most of the guests were arriving, so Drew had to lean down close to her ear to be heard. "Would you like something to drink?"

She smiled back and nodded. "Champagne, please."

"Come this way." He kept her arm in the crook of his and guided her to a table almost at the front of the stage. Two place cards there read "Mr. & Mrs. Rhett Butler." He pulled out her chair for her as she stared at him, openmouthed.

"Stay here, I'll be right back with drinks." He winked at her through his mask and was gone.

She watched in awe as so many beautiful people moved around, chatting and drinking and finding their seats. She tried to count the tables in the room, doing the math at twenty-five hundred a head to see just how much this shindig was bringing in. She didn't think she could ever get used to living in a world where money flowed this freely. What she could do with the five thousand dollars Drew had paid for these seats . . .

He was suddenly back, a champagne flute in each hand. Other people were now starting to arrive at their table, and she wasn't sure how she was expected to interact with them. Drew sat down beside her, placing her drink in front of her. As if he could sense her nervousness, he leaned over and whispered into her ear, "Just be yourself."

She wasn't quite sure what that meant. "Herself" was Hannah. To him, she was Scarlett. So, she just plastered a smile on her face and made small talk with the woman seated to her left about the flowers and her dress. When she looked up, the entire table was full. Drew seemed to know the gentleman sitting across from him and was deep in conversation. *Hmm, so much for being incognito.* A waiter walked by with a tray of champagne, so she waved him over and exchanged her empty glass for a full one. It was so delicious she could hardly help it if the first one went down so easily.

She felt Drew's hand rest on her thigh, and then his fingers slowly inching the fabric of her dress up her leg. When it was high enough, his hand slid onto her bare thigh and rested there, his fingers slowly rubbing back and forth. She glanced around the table nervously, hoping no one could see her raised skirt. Just how far north was his hand going to go? As if he could read her mind, his hand started trailing farther up her leg, Drew still deep in conversation with the man across the table as though nothing was happening.

Before things could go much further, she dropped her free hand discreetly under the table and placed it over his, squeezing it in warning. As a rebuttal, he pinched the inside of her leg, quick and hard. She cried out in surprise. *What the hell!* The guests closest to her turned their heads toward her. Drew turned as well and, wearing the slightest of grins, asked, "Are you all right, darling?"

She laughed shakily and addressed the guests at the table. "Sorry, I accidently stepped on my own foot under the table."

She picked up her champagne and, tipping the glass back, finished it off. Drew's hand was continuing its journey north, and she knew now that trying to stop him was useless. She raised her hand again to signal the waiter for another glass of champagne, who brought it immediately.

His lips were suddenly at her ear, murmuring. "I wouldn't have that third glass of champagne, Scarlett. You haven't eaten in quite some time and I wouldn't want you to lose control."

His innuendo was more than clear. Just because she could, eyes locked with his, she picked up the glass of champagne and took a big sip. He raised his eyebrows and tipped his head at her brazen rebuttal, his fingers still moving up her leg until they were at the apex of her thighs. Only a scrap of material covered it as Marco had insisted she could only wear the thong he'd provided to avoid visible panty lines. Drew's finger ran over her pussy before she felt just the slightest bit of pressure on her clit.

She instantly tried to shut her legs, but Drew leaned into her as if to kiss her, instead growling in her ear, "Open your legs, Scarlett. Now."

She turned her head to him, eyes wide, silently trying to appeal to his senses, but he was having none of it. He worked his hand further between her legs, laying his palm flat against her mound, and continued rubbing his middle and forefinger up and down against her clit. The movement instantly brought heat to her core, and her nipples tightened under the silk lining of her dress. She again brought her hand discreetly under the table, placing it on Drew's forearm, and again tried to stop him before anyone else noticed what he was doing.

He leaned over and whispered in her ear, "Your pussy is hot to the touch. Are you sure you want me to stop?"

She turned her head to him and was barely able to whimper, "*Please.*"

He grinned wickedly at her. "Please what? Is that a yes or a no?"

"Please stop or you'll make me come right here," she ground out, lips smiling, teeth gritted.

"Oh, what I wouldn't do to see that." His blue eyes were gleaming under his mask, matching the devilish look on his face, but he complied with her request and slowly slid his hand from between her legs and out of her skirt. Instead of placing his hand back on the table though, he brought his fingers to his nose and inhaled deeply.

He watched as her eyes widened in shock.

"Have I told you how delicious you smell?" He was leaning close to her and talking low enough that no one could hear their conversation. She nodded hotly, any part of her face not hidden by her mask no doubt flushed a deep pink.

"I cannot wait to taste you later." And then he actually popped his fingers into his mouth, sucking on them as he slowly withdrew them, his gaze locked on hers.

A chuckle escaped him as she leaned away and gulped down more champagne, her eyes darting around the table.

"Am I interrupting?" A deep voice questioned from behind them as a large hand clasped onto Drew's shoulder.

A wide smile stretched across Drew's face as he stood up and embraced the man in a tight hug. "Benny! You're here! How did you find me?"

Hannah quickly appraised the new arrival. He was about the same height as Drew but bulkier, packed with a lot of muscle. He was wearing a tuxedo very similar to Drew's but with a standard black bow tie and no mask. His blue eyes reminded her of Drew's, but Ben's equally dark hair was cut much closer to the scalp. Brothers then, had to be. Unlike his brother, when she looked into Benny's eyes, she saw something in them she recognized: grief, anger, exhaustion.

"Please, you're my brother. You don't think I know you, even with a mask on? And don't call me Benny. You know I hate that."

"I know, that's why I do it." Drew laughed and turned toward her. "Ben, meet Scarlett, my date."

She stood and turned to face Drew's brother, extending her hand. Instead of shaking it, he grasped it gently, leaning in close and kissed her on the cheek before letting go. "Scarlett. Very nice to meet you."

He turned toward Drew, head tilted toward Scarlett. "This is a nice surprise." And then he turned his attention back to her. "I hope he's being nice to you. We were beginning to wonder if he remembered how to date."

She raised an eyebrow at him, wondering just how much about his brother he actually knew, but mustered a polite laugh. "Of course, nothing but a gentleman. It's very nice to meet you."

Upon closer inspection, she noticed he was also holding a cane—part of his ensemble?

"Didn't Drew tell you?" he asked.

"Tell me what?"

He raised his left pant leg, exposing a titanium rod fitted into his dress shoe. "I'm a gimp."

She was startled by his bluntness. "I'm sorry. I didn't realize."

"Ben, stop embarrassing her," Drew admonished, then to her, "He likes to make people feel as uncomfortable about it as he does."

Instead of being uncomfortable though, she saw red. "You were in the Middle East, right? Drew did mention that." Venom laced her tone.

"Yes, for three years. Until this." He banged the cane against his metal leg, his anger and frustration over his situation evident.

"Be glad you came home at all. Some people don't. Think about that instead of feeling sorry for yourself," she seethed.

Both men drew back in surprise at her harsh response.

"You think I—" Ben started to respond angrily, but Drew interjected, "Okay, why don't we go get you a drink, Ben?"

Drew started ushering Ben toward the bar but not before

turning back and glaring at her in confusion. "Stay there."

Her pulse was beating fiercely, but she did as he requested and sat back down in her seat. She took a sip of her champagne to calm herself, wishing she had something stronger to drink.

A few minutes of quiet fuming later, the music suddenly stopped, the lights throughout the room dimmed, and the crowd quieted. Only the lights illuminating the stage in front of her remained bright. Then Drew walked across the stage to the podium in the center. *What is he doing up there?* At the podium, he adjusted the microphone and began to speak. She realized he had taken his mask off.

"Ladies and gentleman, I want to welcome you all to the second annual GetVetsSet Charity Masquerade Ball. As many of you know, this is a cause that is extremely personal to me. My brother, Benjamin Sapphire, was an infantryman in the army, supporting our country's efforts in Baghdad, when the vehicle he was in struck an IED. Two men, Ben's brothers in arms, died as a result, and Ben lost his left leg below the knee."

Drew took a deep breath, looked down at the podium for a moment and then cleared his throat before continuing.

"Over time, and with a lot of help from many doctors and nurses, Ben's external injuries were treated and healed. But there were internal injuries that we didn't know how to fix, ones we couldn't see, but that every soldier coming home, injured or not, experiences. Not until my brother almost took his life did he get the help and support he needed."

Her breath caught in her throat. She'd misjudged Ben and his attitude at his injury and felt regret at the way she had spoken to him. She turned her focus back to Drew, understanding fully the struggle he must have felt over his brother's plight.

There was a long pause before he continued, "Twenty-two. Twenty-two seems like a comparatively small number, right?"

Drew looked out over the crowd, shaking his head in disgust as the passion in his voice increased.

"Well, that's the number of soldiers that commit suicide every day. Twenty-two mothers, fathers, wives, brothers, sisters, sons and daughters that have to struggle with the death of their loved one. When you add that up, it's a staggering loss. One that we hope our organization, GetVetsSet, will help to eliminate entirely."

A loud round of applause echoed throughout the ballroom. She stared in awe at Drew and this side of him that she had no idea how to reconcile with the rest. They had far more in common than either of them were probably aware of. Drew waved at the crowd to quiet them again.

"At GetVetsSet, we have created programs to help veterans regain their mental, physical and emotional well-being. And tonight, each one of you, through your generous donations, has helped us raise just over one million dollars to continue building programs and supporting our veterans. I'll personally be matching that donation with another million. Thank you so much. Please give yourself a big round of applause and enjoy the rest of your evening. You've earned it!"

The room broke out in a loud roar of applause and cheers as Drew made his way offstage, down a set of stairs. It was then that she saw Ben standing at the bottom of them. Drew pulled him into a tight embrace, holding him for a long moment and speaking something into his ear before letting go and walking away.

Hannah was forced to look away when plates full of food

appeared before her, and she lost track of Drew in the crowd milling at the foot of the stage. She didn't want to start without him and searched the stage area, then the bar for him, but didn't see him. She'd just turned back in her seat and was taking a sip of her champagne when she felt a tap on her shoulder. Ben. She stood instantly, wanting to apologize for her earlier actions.

"Ben, I'm sorry if I spoke rudely to you before. It's just that—" Hannah started, but he stopped her with a raised hand.

"Forget about it. I don't know your story and you don't know mine." He ran a hand through his short hair, baring a tattoo that edged from under his shirtsleeve onto the top of his hand: a black rose with a gold oak leaf. The familiarity of it sent goose bumps across her arms. If she raised his sleeve, the words "Never Forget" would be scripted above the rose.

She looked at him curiously, dragging her gaze away from the tattoo. "I'd like to hear your story sometime."

He scoffed. "Yeah, maybe another time. Right now, Drew wants you to meet him on the terrace." Ben pointed toward a set of curtained glass doors to the side of the stage and then walked away, using his cane as support, not waiting for her response. She made her way to the terrace doors, stepped through and closed them behind her.

Drew stood quietly in the shadows as he watched Scarlett make her way across the terrace. A light breeze swirled around her, the skirt of her dress flowing behind her as she seemed to glide over the marble stones. He wondered about the sharp reaction she'd had toward Ben and what had triggered it. There must be a story there to evoke such a response from her.

"Drew?" Scarlett called his name and stopped walking. He watched her turn in a circle, enjoying the way she moved her body, before he stepped out of the shadows and came up behind her.

"Hey." She started in surprise as he wrapped his arms around her waist and nuzzled her neck, inhaling her floral scent.

"You scared me!" She laughed. "I didn't know where you were."

"I was watching you." He tightened his embrace before whispering in her ear, "I like how you move."

Her cheeks rose up in a smile. Instead of replying, she twisted in his arms to face him, eyes framed by the silk and diamonds in her mask, and brought her lips up to his in a hungry kiss. He swept his tongue across her bottom lip before sliding it into her mouth, the kiss becoming more urgent as their breaths became one with each other. He guided her backward, never breaking their kiss, until he felt her bump up against the railing surrounding the terrace.

Tearing his lips from hers, he planted hot kisses down the length of her neck until he reached the swell of her breast, now heaving with her panting breaths. He slid the silk of her dress off one breast, exposing her nipple, and then ran his tongue over it, watching it peak as the cold air hit its wetness. Scarlett sighed loudly, and his cock grew harder, straining against his trousers. He skimmed his hand down the length of her body until he reached her thigh, and then, grasping her firmly, brought her leg up and wrapped it around him, pressing his raging erection up against her core.

"Ohhh, Drew . . ." Scarlett breathed as he continued to rock himself against her. He pushed her skirt up and over his leg, clearing the thin barrier between them, and then pushed the flimsy fabric of her panties out of the way before sliding his finger over her pussy.

"Oh my god baby, you're soaking wet." His voice came out

rough as he fought to control the urge to bend her over the railing and fuck her senseless.

"That's because you keep teasing me." Scarlett was looking at him, her eyes bright with desire, her response laced in want.

He smiled back at her, almost feral. "I can't help it. You're doing something to me. You've cast some kind of spell on me."

He rocked himself into her again and then abruptly dropped her leg, smoothing her skirt back down. As much as he wanted to fuck her right here and now, anyone could walk onto the terrace at any moment. He didn't want to risk exposing her like that. He leaned forward and kissed her deeply, then took a step back from her.

"Do you want to get out of here?"

"But we haven't even eaten or danced yet."

He kissed her lightly on the lips again. "I'll feed you. And if you want to dance, we can do that too. I just want to be with you. I don't want to share you with everyone here. I've done what I needed to do here."

A slow smile spread across her face as she answered timidly, "Okay."

He took her hand then and, entwining his fingers with hers, led her back to the terrace doors she had entered from.

"I need to grab my clutch. I left it on the table," she said as they made their way through the doors.

"Okay. I'd like to try and find Ben and say good-bye as well. Let's grab your clutch first and try the bar. That's usually where he can be found." He knew from experience that Benny had either left after his speech or was drowning his aversion to these types of social events in whiskey.

After retrieving her bag, they made their way to the bar, his hand still holding hers. As they approached, Scarlett pulled him to a stop, pointing to the restrooms off to their right.

"Do you mind? I'll only be a minute?"

"Of course not. Go ahead and just meet me at the bar when you're done. I'll wait there for you." He leaned over and kissed her softly on the lips, releasing her hand but not his attention.

"What?" she asked in apparent confusion.

"Nothing." Drew smiled seductively. "I want to watch you walk in that dress again. Is that okay?"

She smiled demurely as she turned and walked away, rolling her hips as she went.

Hannah quickly took care of business and then made her way to the lounge area of the ladies' room so she could freshen her face up a bit. She loved the mask but was tired of its confines, and it was making her face sweaty, so she untied it. They were leaving and Drew had removed his, so she must be safe. Besides, it's not like anyone could know she was his *paid* date. She touched up her powder and reapplied her lipstick. Miraculously, her hair seemed to have survived the mask, as well as the little make-out session she and Drew had just indulged in. Karla had definitely done an amazing job on her hair. She took the mask and, folding it delicately in half, placed it in her clutch.

As she walked up to the bar, she scanned the area for Drew and found him near the end. Instead of speaking with Ben, he seemed to have found the attention of a rather busty, if not attractive, redhead in a tight black dress. Jealousy instantly flared, surprising her, igniting her bold approach.

"Hello, Drew." She sidled up against him tightly, wrapping her arm around his waist and her hand on his chest before placing a kiss on his cheek. She turned to the redhead, extending her hand. "I'm Scarlett. Drew's date."

The woman eyed her up and down, a look of distaste stretched over her features. Drew chuckled under his breath, which only raised Hannah's hackles further. Ignoring her hand, the redhead turned toward Drew, eyebrows raised in obvious disappointment. "You brought a date?"

Hannah felt some relief at the woman's response—and at the confirmation of Drew's earlier confession about not dating. Though . . . he might have previously *slept* with the woman. She certainly wasn't hiding her disappointment well at Drew bringing a date.

"Yes, I brought a date. And we were just leaving." Drew dismissed her politely, and then turned to Hannah. "Come, let's go, apparently Ben has already left." Then, to the redhead, "Have a good night."

Unable to contain her curiosity—because lord knew she had no right to be jealous, right?—Hannah waited until they were away from the bar before pulling Drew to a stop. "Who was that woman?"

An almost satisfied grin broke out across his face before he responded, "Scarlett, are you jealous?"

She was about to respond when a hand reached out and tapped her arm. "It is you! Harold, come see. I told you it was her!"

Drew looked on in surprise as an elderly woman, bathed in jewels, addressed Scarlett with such familiarity. The stranger beckoned someone Drew could only assume was her husband over to see Scarlett.

"Mrs. Downing! Hello, how are you?" Scarlett bussed the

elderly woman on her cheek. "And Mr. Downing, hello! You look so handsome in your tuxedo."

Drew stood back in shock as he realized she was addressing Harold Downing. *The* Harold Downing, who owned one of the wealthiest brokerage houses in the country. Scarlett seemed to be full of surprises.

"My dear, look how beautiful you are this evening!" Mr. Downing had reached Scarlett and was kissing her on the cheek. "How nice to see you out and about and out of the shop."

"Thank you so much. You both look lovely as well." Scarlett glanced at Drew with what could only be described as sheer panic on her face, clearly unsure what to do next. While he was extremely curious to learn more about this shop Scarlett worked at, he'd better rescue her before she imploded. He extended his hand.

"Mr. Downing, I presume?" And smiled widely. "Andrew Sapphire. Very nice to meet you. I've heard so much about you. It's nice to finally meet the man in the flesh."

He took Drew's hand and shook it vigorously. "Ah, the same could be said about you, young man. Please, call me Harold. Wonderful speech this evening. Hope you're taking good care of this young lady here. She's a very special girl."

Drew looked at Scarlett, who was still vibrating with nerves, and then back at Mr. Downing. Perhaps he could take advantage of this situation and learn a bit more about her . . . "Yes, I agree, quite special. How do you two know each other?"

But much to Drew's disappointment, Mrs. Downing interrupted then and tried to unobtrusively lead her husband away. "Harold, let's go and leave these two lovebirds to their evening."

"Oh, Alice! Give me a few minutes with the man." He tried to shoo his wife away.

Yes, Drew thought to himself, *give me a few more minutes*. Much to his surprise, Scarlett spoke up, placing her hand on Drew's arm.

"Actually, we were just on our way out. Drew has an emergency that needs his attention."

Her small hand gripped his arm with white knuckles. He was crossing a line with her that he shouldn't be. Instantly, he put his hand over hers in a conciliatory fashion.

"Oh, yes." Harold started nodding. "I know all about those." He turned his attention toward Scarlett then. "I'm sure I'll see you later this week at the shop, dear."

Mrs. Downing turned towards Drew then to wish him a goodnight. "So nice to see our girl out with someone. Hope you're both able to enjoy the rest of your evening."

Drew had to strain to hear Harold's conspiratorial whisper as the man drew closer to Scarlett. "I think I want to do something different this week for Alice." The old man gave Scarlett a wink then and kissed her on the cheek.

"Of course, I look forward to it." She patted him on the hand and then his wife. "Mrs. Downing, it was so nice to see you."

"You know I always love seeing you dear. Have a nice evening." And with that, Mr. Downing took his wife's hand, placing it in the crook of his arm, and led her away.

Drew raised his eyebrows at Scarlett. "The Downings? You know the Downings?"

She started walking toward the exit again. "Don't think you can change the subject on me. I want to know who that woman was."

"Wait a minute. You know one of the wealthiest couples in the country, and I'm not allowed to ask about it?"

She stopped walking and turned to look at him. "No, you don't. You get Scarlett. That's all you get. You don't get anything else from me."

Dumbfounded, he just looked at her, reality slapping him in the face. This woman had only shared a small piece of herself, and everything else was a complete mystery to him. He had so many questions about her: Why was her reaction to his brother so intense, who was the "we" she'd referred to with such a warm smile on her face at lunch, and why, if she associated with people like the Downings, was she selling herself at auction? That one small piece wasn't going to be enough. He wanted more.

Chapter Nine

Hannah stood in silent thought as Drew gave the ticket to the valet driver. Neither of them had said anything to each other after her last comment. She was still in a bit of shock at running into the Downings. She'd known there would be a slight risk at seeing someone she knew here and had realized, a bit too late, that she should have left her mask on until they'd left. It wasn't that she was ashamed to be with Drew, but she needed to keep her personal life separate from this choice she'd made. Seeing the Downings reminded her how precariously close she'd come to exposing that life.

"You're shivering." Drew came up behind her and placed his jacket over her shoulders, running his hands down the length of her arms before stepping away.

"Thank you." His warmth still lingered on the fabric that surrounded her and she pulled it more tightly around herself. She leaned down and inhaled deeply, taking in his scent as it drifted up from the jacket. She loved the comfort that his warmth and scent were bringing her, and hated herself at the same time for it.

The valet drove up with Drew's car, stopping directly in front of them. He jumped out and ran around to open the door for her, but Drew was already there. He held her hand as she sat down, and she wrapped her skirt around her legs before he shut the door. In less than a minute, he was in the car and pulling away from the hotel.

He turned on the radio, settling on something acoustic. She listened for a moment but didn't recognize the artist.

"This is lovely. Who is it?"

"Jason Mraz. Do you know him?"

She shook her head. "I think I know some of his songs. Not this one though. I like it."

"Yes, just simple. It eases me."

They rode in silence for a few more moments until she realized they weren't heading back in the direction of the estate.

"Where are we going?"

"It's a surprise." He looked over at her, his voice low. "Do you trust me?"

"Are you going to tell me who that redhead was?" She wasn't forgetting about that bitch anytime soon.

"Are you going to tell me about the Downings? 'Cause I'm dying to know."

"Drew, I can't. I'm sorry." She sighed. "I'm not trying to be difficult. Really. But that part of my life isn't part of this life."

Drew was silent for a few moments before responding. "Okay, Scarlett. I understand, but I'm not going to lie; I hate it. I'm usually the one in control,   but I feel like you're holding all the cards here."

"No, I'm not. You paid for this part of me. You paid for Scarlett. I'm sorry, but this is all I can give you."

"Maybe that's not enough," he gritted out under his breath.

She turned her head toward him in surprise. "Drew . . ." She faltered, not even sure what to say. If she was honest with herself, hearing him say he wanted more was a relief. To know she wasn't alone in her confusion about her growing feelings for him. She couldn't deny that she was beginning to feel more for him than she should.

"Don't." He held his hand up and responded before she could try and continue. "It's okay, Scarlett. I'm being unfair to you. Besides, it's only 9:30. I have you, or at least I have Scarlett, for another eighteen hours. Let's just try and enjoy that."

"Okay." She was silent for the next few moments and just listened to the music flowing through the car's speakers. They seemed to be heading east, away from the city.

"Are you going to tell me where we're going yet?"

He smiled. "My house in The Hamptons. Are you okay with that? I can still have you back at the estate by early morning."

"Your house?" she squeaked. "Is that even allowed? I mean, I know the masquerade ball was one thing, but your house?"

He scoffed. "What's the worst that can happen? Domme Maria kicks me out of Timide? It's not the only club in town."

She looked at him in surprise. "You would risk your membership to bring me to your house?"

"I hardly think my membership is in any real danger. We're supposed to be at a ball. As far as anyone knows, that's where we are. Who is to know any differently unless we tell them? Besides, I think the money I spend there would be greatly missed."

"Well it's nice to know my worth, I guess."

"Scarlett, don't." He glanced over at her, longing in his voice. "I want to share this with you. It's one of my favorite places."

What could she say to that? Besides, she was tired of fighting over what she should and shouldn't be feeling, or doing, or caring about. She bent her head down, kissing the palm of his hand. "Okay."

"Okay?" he asked in relief.

"Okay." She laughed. "Just tell me it's not too much farther though, cause I'm starving!"

"In that case," he shifted the car into a higher gear and punched the gas, "I'll get us there as fast as I can."

"What kind of car is this anyway?"

He smiled broadly. "It's a Jaguar. An F-Type S Coupe."

She shook her head, grinning. "Boys and their cars."

A little over an hour later, Drew pulled off the road onto a long, white gravel driveway. As the house came into view, Scarlett gasped, her eyes open wide, awe evident on her face. He beamed with pride over her delight. He'd recently had it built, and although it had been designed to be modern, he'd striven to balance cutting-edge with warmth and an inviting presence.

It was a large, contemporary home made up of natural wood and large floor-to-ceiling windows. The windows on the lower floor were glowing a rich yellow, and beyond the house, a rolling, manicured lawn met a pristine white beach, waves lapping lightly against its edge.

"Drew, this is gorgeous!"

"Wait till you see the inside."

He jumped out and came around to open her door and help her out of the car.

"Careful. It's all stone gravel here and probably won't be easy to maneuver in your heels."

Scarlett stepped out of the car and tried to balance on the balls of her feet, tiptoeing over the gravel toward the entrance. Before she got three steps, he swept her up in his arms, a quick yelp of surprise escaping from her, and carried her the rest of the way.

"Sorry, this just seemed easier." He dropped a kiss on her nose as he went. She simply smiled in response and then rested her head on his shoulder.

Once inside, he placed her gently down in the entryway. He took in her perusal of his home, trying to ascertain her opinion. He'd had the inside designed to be light and airy, the walls a soft white, the floors a light-colored hardwood. Her gaze focused on the floor-to-ceiling windows that spanned the width of the living room, framing a view of the ocean beyond.

"Drew, it's lovely." She turned toward him.

"I'll give you a tour later, but let's go to the kitchen and see if we can find something to eat."

He walked down the hallway into a large open space that contained the kitchen and living room. The kitchen was modern and sleek but had clearly been customized for a man with its natural wood paneling and butcher block. Stainless steel appliances and light fixtures complemented the wood and white marble countertop. Drew started pulling things out of the large fridge and placing them on the butcher block.

"Let's see," he mumbled as he placed each item down. "Brie, grapes, chicken, marinated mushrooms, blueberries, some olives." He turned and looked at her. "Does any of this look good?"

She laughed. "It all looks good! I'm so hungry!"

He pointed at one of the cabinets. "Okay, why don't you grab some plates while I go down and grab a bottle of wine for us?"

"Perfect." Scarlett walked around the counter and opened the cabinet, grabbing two plates for them. He left her and walked around the corner and downstairs to a small room that contained his wine cellar. He picked a white and a red and made his way back to the living room.

He came around the corner with the two bottles of wine just as she finished taking her shoes off. A wide grin spread across his face in joy and surprise as he took in the setting she had created for them. Instead of the kitchen, on the small coffee table in the living room, plates, glasses, silverware, the food and even a couple of candles all were waiting for him.

"I wasn't sure if you wanted red or white, so I grabbed one of each." He put the bottles down on the counter and moved to one of the drawers for an opener.

"I'd love a glass of the red. Are you okay eating in here?"

"It's absolutely perfect." He beamed back at her, while opening the bottle of red before carrying it over to their make-shift picnic spot. He poured each of them a glass before sitting down.

"I hope you don't mind this little smorgasbord. It's quick and easy and no cooking required."

"Are you kidding?" she responded as she popped a grape in her mouth. "This is so perfect. I love food you can eat with your fingers."

He smiled and watched Scarlett as she pulled a piece of chicken breast off the roaster and put it in her mouth, chewing happily. *She just might be perfect.* The thought struck him like a bolt of lightening, jarring him to his core. He hadn't felt anything like this, since, well, maybe ever. Dinners with his ex-wife had always been formal affairs. The thought of her sitting cross-legged, in a ball gown no less, blissfully eating chicken with her fingers was a foreign one. His ex-wife would send a meal back to the kitchen if a stray pea rolled into her starch, berating the service of the restaurant as inadequate and appalling. He took a big gulp of wine to calm the beating of his heart as the reality of his growing feelings became more evident.

"Do you want me to make a plate for you?" Scarlett asked, pulling him out of his scattered thoughts.

He shook his head. "No, no. I'm good. I'm just going to pick like you." He grabbed the drumstick on the chicken, twisting it off and taking a bite. For the next few moments they both just ate in silence. He liked watching Scarlett's expressions change with each bite of food. She closed her eyes in delight with the blueberries and scrunched her nose up while trying some of the saltier olives. When she brought the wineglass to her lips and took her first sip, she closed her eyes and moaned loudly.

"You like?" he asked, laughing.

"Oh my god. This is so unbelievably good. It's warm and smooth and tastes like peppered blackberries."

He smiled again at how easily she was satisfied. "Have you had enough to eat?"

"Yes, I'm good. Thank you. Do you want me to clean up?" Hannah started to stand so she could clear their mess, but Drew grabbed her hand and stood up beside her.

"Leave it. I thought maybe we could take a walk on the beach."

She looked out the windows at the waves lapping against the shore and nodded, a smile breaking across her face. "I'd love that."

Drew led her from the living room and through a side door in the kitchen out onto a large deck. He stopped and pulled off his shoes and socks, then continued across the deck and down some stairs. At the bottom, he threw a switch mounted on one of the deck posts, and lights appeared before them, trailing down a pathway that led to the beach.

As he took her hand and started walking down the path, the ocean breeze nipped pleasantly at her exposed skin. "Are you cold at all? I can go back in and get you a blanket if so."

She shook her head. "No, I'm okay right now."

The path meandered down a small hill before opening onto the beach. The moon was high and full above them, reflected off the water's waves. She stopped and marveled at the view in front of her.

"Oh, Drew, this is absolutely gorgeous. No wonder you love it here." She turned to look at him. He was staring out at the waves, a small, content smile on his face.

"Yeah, this is where I come to just be me. It's my quiet place. I love it here."

"Thank you for sharing it with me." She rose up and kissed him softly on the lips.

"Come on. Let's walk a bit." Hand in hand, they strolled down to the water's edge and then followed it down the beach for about a half mile before turning back.

Her dress trailed behind her in the sand. The waves lapped rhythmically against the shoreline.

She eventually broke the silence. "Tell me why this is your favorite place."

He smiled down at her as they continued walking. "My parents have a much larger house on the beach, but it's in California. It's so far north that it's almost in Oregon. It's a town called Crescent City. Anyway, we didn't go all that often, as my father was always busy working or traveling, but when we would go . . ."

She looked over to see Drew's eyes closed as he relayed his memories to her. "This place reminds me of those simpler times.

Happy times. Ben and I would play all day on that beach. When we were little, it was making sand castles and chasing seagulls or wakeboarding. When we were older, it was surfing and chasing girls."

She laughed with him at the memory. "I can totally see the two of you in action back then. I bet none of those girls had a chance!"

"Actually, we were the ones that usually ended up with the broken hearts. But, oh what fun we had getting them. It's actually where I met my ex-wife."

She was unable to mask the surprise on her face. "I think that's the first time I've heard you speak fondly of her."

He raised his eyebrows in thought. "Hmm. I guess so."

He was quiet a few minutes before continuing. "It wasn't always bad between us. We were happy when we were younger. When I didn't have so many of the responsibilities I ended up growing into and could focus more of my attention on her."

"It's okay, Drew, you don't have to explain." She didn't want to make him feel uncomfortable.

"No, it's okay. The demise of our marriage is probably more my fault than hers anyway. We loved each other very much at one time, but I took that for granted when my father demanded more of me, pulling my focus in another direction. She tried, I think she really did. But ultimately, she was just too lonely."

"You sound sad about that."

"Let's just say I've worked hard not to put myself in that position again."

"Is that why you entertain this sort of lifestyle now?" Hannah mused.

"This sort of lifestyle? What sort is that, Scarlett?" he asked, not harshly, but curiously.

"I don't know. I guess the kind where you pay for someone to keep you company. No commitment."

"Unfortunately, I wasn't the one with the commitment issue," he scoffed. "She was. But, again, if I had paid more attention, listened to her, maybe things would have been different. Maybe we were just too young."

She squeezed his hand in response and pulled him to a stop. "I'm sorry. I didn't mean to upset you. I was just trying to understand."

"It's okay. I get it. I'm probably not the easiest guy to understand."

They both turned and continued walking down the beach, angling back toward the house looming in the distance now.

"What about you?" he asked quietly.

"What about me?"

"Were you ever married?"

For a long time, she couldn't answer. Drew stopped and pulled her close, looking at her questioningly.

"Scarlett?"

She looked down at the ground, absently noticing the sand that had gathered around the long hem of her dress. She sighed. "You don't get to ask me these kinds of questions. I'm sorry."

"Why can't I ask you these kinds of questions? I just told you all about my marriage. Is it wrong for me to want to get to know you better?" Frustration was evident in his voice and the tightened features of his face.

"What difference does it make? I'm yours for one weekend." She looked down at the ground again before continuing. "But—of course if I was married, I wouldn't be standing here with you right now."

Drew pulled her tight against him, forcing her to lift her face to his. "I don't know why it matters to me, Scarlett, but it does. You make me want things and feel things I haven't felt in a very long time. I want to know you, all of you."

Drew could see the confusion and angst in her face, eyebrows scrunched up in worry. To stop her from responding, he kissed her. Long and sweet and torturously slow to try and make them both forget what he'd just admitted. Or maybe to confirm it.

When he broke them apart, instead of continuing the conversation, he turned, grabbed her hand and pulled her down the beach closer to the house, his long strides challenging her to keep up. "Come on. I think I promised you some dancing."

She laughed. "What?"

He looked back at her and smiled. "Remember? On the terrace, you said we hadn't gotten to eat or dance."

"Yes?"

"Well, I've fed you. Now I need to make sure you get to dance. We can't let that dress go to waste, can we?"

She pointed down at the muddy hem of the dress and cringed. "I'm not sure you're going to want this messy dress sliding all over your beautiful floors."

He stopped, taking in the hem, noticing for the first time that it was indeed quite muddy. He shrugged and smiled. "Oh well. I don't mind if you don't."

She couldn't help but smile back at him. "Well, all right then! Let's go dance!"

They made it back to the house and entered through the doorway they had exited earlier. Drew wiped his feet off before helping Scarlett shake as much of the sand off her dress as she could. He took her hand and led her to the back of the house where the library was located.

"This room is gorgeous! I would never leave it if I lived here."

He radiated pride as he searched through the songs on the digital music player set into one of the shelves. He knew exactly which song he wanted . . . "I didn't want a traditional library. I wanted one bright and full of light. I'm glad you like it."

She walked over to the window, pressing her hand flat on the cool surface of the glass, and the moonlight coming through the window silhouetted her frame. As the room filled with the music he'd selected just for her, he grabbed her free hand and pulled her into his arms. She laughed when she heard what song he had chosen. He spun her around, and they both sang along with the music as they danced.

Scarlett was laughing, jumping up and down as she took in his crazy dancing. "Oh my god, Drew! Seriously?"

"What? This is the perfect song for you and those beautiful eyes!" He grasped her hand again and twirled her this way and that, her dress swinging up and around, revealing her up on tiptoes. "I love Van Morrison, and Brown-Eyed Girl is a classic!"

As quickly as the song started, it seemed to end. They both stopped, breathing hard from their silly dancing, grinning wide at each other. The lyrics from the next song crooned much slower than the first. Drew gathered Scarlett in his arms and started swaying to the music, singing the lyrics to Crazy Love quietly in her ear while they moved.

With each turn, Drew's hand, placed low and flat on Hannah's back, pulled her in closer, so that their bodies felt almost like one.

His heart beat heavily under her hand as it lay against his chest, and his breath tickled against her ear as he sang. She didn't dare look up at him, afraid of what might come next in this intimate moment they were sharing.

The song came to an end. He dropped his hold around her waist and took her hand. "Come."

It was all he said before walking out of the room, leaving the next song to play as he led her up a staircase and then down a hallway. At the end of the hallway, he opened a door and pulled her into what must be the master bedroom. One exterior wall held the same floor-to-ceiling windows as the rooms below, overlooking the ocean. The room was simply furnished. A king-sized bed sat against the back wall, and a natural wood dresser and wardrobe rested against the two other walls. The floors were a light wood, soft and warm on her feet, and a white fur rug lay in the center.

Drew closed the door and turned toward her. Without saying a word, he slid his fingers down her arms, then pulled her hands up and over her head. He held her like that, delicately, with one hand and used the other to pull down the zipper on the side of her dress. Then he released her hands, letting them fall back to her sides, and pushed the single strap holding up her dress slowly off her shoulder, causing the entire dress to slip down and off her body. He slid her thong down her legs until it fell to the floor.

She stood before him, naked, with only the diamond choker and cuff bracelet adorning her body. He stepped back and gazed at her, lust and desire evident in his dark blue eyes. She stepped forward, out of the dress and panties pooled on the floor, and waited for his next command. It didn't come. Instead, he unbuttoned and removed his shirt as he slowly walked around her, his eyes never leaving her body.

Her nipples grew tight under his gaze, and though he hadn't even touched her, his scorching look caused her body to flare in heat and wetness to pool at her core. Her fingers tingled with the desire to touch him and run them over his lean, muscled body.

As he stopped in front of her again, he unfastened his belt and then the button holding up his trousers, his gaze still locked on her body. In one motion, he bent over and slid off his trousers. When he stood up, his cock jutted hard and long against his stomach.

Still not having said a word, he slowly walked up to her again. This time, he placed his hand flat on her stomach, leaving it there as he walked around to the back of her and then pulled her flush against his front. His other hand snaked up and around her neck to finger the collar of diamond lace that encircled it while his head leaned down against hers. She heard him inhale deeply—was he smelling her?—and his lips pressed against her ear.

"You are so fucking gorgeous." And then he spun her around and pressed his lips to hers in a heated kiss. Her arms wrapped up and around his neck, then further up to grip his hair as their kiss intensified. As his tongue invaded her mouth and his teeth nipped at her lips, he slowly pushed her backward until her legs met the foot of the bed. Instead of pushing her down, he broke the kiss, bent down and picked her up under the legs, cradling her like a child before walking around to the side of the bed and setting her down in the middle of it.

He trailed his hands down the length of her body as he rose and moved back to the end of the bed. He kneeled and, as he bent down, captured her ankle in his hand, raising her leg to meet his lips. Starting at her ankle, his lips left a scorching trail of heat up the length of her leg as he made his way up her body. When he reached the juncture of her legs, he kissed her there sweetly before continuing up and along her stomach to her breasts. He dragged his tongue across the tip of each nipple and then ever so slowly took one of the peaks into his mouth and sucked.

Hannah's back arched off the bed as his mouth latched onto her, and her hands grasped onto his head, not wanting him to roam further. Drew continued to suck and lave her breast for a few moments before moving to the other. She moaned at the intense pleasure, the slow, sensual pace of his exploration of her body leaving every inch of her on fire.

When his attention to the second breast was complete, he peppered soft, wet kisses over her clavicle and down the inside of her arm. When he reached the diamond cuff on her wrist, his fingers trailed over it, encircling it delicately before raising her hand to his lips, placing a kiss on her palm, all the while gazing passionately into her eyes.

"Drew . . ." she whispered, not knowing how much more of this sensual intensity she could take.

Drew shifted his body fully over Scarlett's, his elbows on either side of her head, and lowered his mouth to hers in a searing kiss. Her hands snaked up and around his neck, fingers wide around his head, trying to pull him in closer, deeper as his tongue invaded her mouth. He gradually lowered his body until he was seated between her legs. His cock was hard and throbbing as it lay against her wet center. As he continued to kiss her, he used one hand to guide himself into her heat. Their mouths both opened wide as he slid all the way in, their heads thrown back in shared ecstasy. He brought his hands up and cradled each side of Scarlett's face, his eyes locked on hers as he began to rock in and out of her.

Her hands moved down to grasp his ass, fingernails digging in as she urged him to go deeper and harder with each thrust. Sweat dripped off his forehead and landed on her cheek. Each of them moaning in pleasure. Scarlett started to close her eyes and throw her head back, but his grasp tightened around her face. He wanted to see her, to know if she was feeling what he was, to know it wasn't just him.

"No, Scarlett," he breathed. "Eyes open. I want to see you come apart."

Her only response was a low, guttural moan. He increased his thrusts, pushing harder, but not faster. Scarlett's fingernails dug even deeper in his ass as she grasped onto him in response. Her body climbed toward its release, all of her muscles beginning to tighten around him. He let go of one side of her face to grab her leg below the knee, lifting it, pushing himself even deeper.

"Yes! Yes, like that!" she moaned. "God, don't stop, Drew!"

She tried to thrash her head back and forth, but Drew managed to hold it firmly with one hand, never unlocking his gaze from hers. As she came apart, he thrust hard one final time, joining her in oblivion, and watched as her eyes rolled back in her head. He crashed his lips down on hers, tasting everything his desire brought her, and his cock jerked inside her one last time.

He pulled his lips away, both of them gasping as he did, eyes meeting and holding for a moment before he slid away and rolled to his side. He pulled Scarlett with him, nestling her against him as he wrapped his arms around her. His hands were over her heart, and he could feel it beating quickly as it recovered from their lovemaking.

Chapter Ten

Hannah's fingers grazed back and forth over the dark hair sprinkling Drew's forearm as she tried to understand what had just happened. That hadn't been just fucking. Where were the rope and spankings and punishments that had been promised? These weren't the actions of a Dominant controlling a submissive for his pleasure. The way he'd just made love to her—yes, it *had* felt like love—sent her mind racing. This entire weekend had been anything but what she had expected. She was in disbelief that she had been in Drew's company for only thirty hours. She couldn't deny their connection: it felt as if she had known him forever.

"What are you thinking about?" he murmured into her hair. "I can hear your mind going a million miles a minute."

She didn't dare tell him what she was really thinking. "Nothing, really. Just relaxing."

"Please tell me your real name," he asked softly.

She remained quiet for a moment, unsure of what to say, not wanting to ruin the intimacy of what they had just shared. "I can't, Drew. You know that."

"Why? Why can't you tell me? What harm would it cause?" Frustration was evident in his voice.

"Because I just . . . I can't. My life outside of this world is my own, and I need to keep it that way."

He sighed. "Then tell me something that I *can* know. I want to know who *you* are, not Scarlett."

She sighed deeply because she understood what he wanted, and there was even a piece of her that wanted to share everything she was with him. But there was a bigger piece, the piece she needed to keep safe from this world, that drove her decisions.

"Okay, I'll make a deal with you. I'll ask you a question that I think is acceptable. If you want, you can ask me the same question back."

"If that's what you're willing to give me, then I'll take it. Go."

"Let's start out with an easy one. How old are you?"

"I'm thirty-four. You?" Drew returned.

"I'm twenty-seven."

"Huh, I would have guessed twenty-three or twenty-four."

"I guess I'll appreciate that in a few years." She laughed, feeling the mood lighten already. "Okay, what's your favorite food?"

"Oh jeez. I like so many things. I guess if I have to pick my absolute favorite, I'll go with the manly answer and say a good steak."

"So typical!" She squeezed his hand. "Favorite movie?"

"Uh-uh. You didn't tell me your favorite food," he countered.

"Oh yeah, sorry. I love pasta. Any kind. I could eat it every day. But then I'd probably weigh an extra fifty pounds, so I treat myself to it once a week. So, favorite movie?"

"I don't know about that one." He thought for a moment. "I guess *The Godfather*?"

"God, Drew, could you be any more of a typical man?" she joked.

"So, then, tell me yours."

"It's *Pride and Prejudice*. But the one with Keira Knightley. There's about ten versions of that movie by now."

"Um yeah, speaking of typical choices— 'Scarlett'?" Drew mused.

"I know, I know. Hmmm, okay, let's step this up a notch," she said. "Okay, who was your best friend growing up?"

"That's easy. Benny. We did everything together. That guy knows more about me than I care to admit. Okay, now you. Who was your best friend?"

"Cathy. We met when I was in third grade. My family had just moved to town and we were seated next to each other. I was terrified. She was so nice to me. The teacher assigned us to do a science project together, and we picked monarch butterflies as our subject. We bonded over chasing them in a field by her house."

"Are you still friends?"

"Yes, I suppose we are. I don't see her much but we keep up through Facebook. God, we grew up together, swimming in streams, writing notes, singing silly songs and of course chasing boys." She laughed at the memories.

"That sounds nice. Where did you grow up?"

"Nope. I get to ask the questions! Not you!" she chastised.

"Okay, okay! Sorry!" He held his hands up in surrender. "Do you want something to drink?"

She sat up and faced him. "That actually sounds great."

"Okay, sit tight. I'll be back." Drew jumped up from the bed and left the room. Relief surged through her. Not because he was gone, but because he seemed to be content with this getting-to-know-you game. As quickly as the relief came, it left again. She was developing feelings for Drew. It mattered to her what he thought and how he felt.

And she knew from his actions and his questions that he was feeling something for her too. *I mean, he brought me on a date.* Something he hadn't done for years. But it was also obvious that his business was his life. Although she had to question how much of it had been forced upon him by his father.

While these thoughts swirled in her mind, she got up and opened a few drawers on the dresser until she came across one filled with T-shirts. She grabbed one and pulled it over her head. It fell halfway down her thighs and looked more like a dress, but it was soft and comfy and, best of all, it smelled like Drew.

"Cute." He was standing in the doorway, holding the bottle of wine from earlier and their glasses.

"I hope you don't mind. I didn't want to put that dress back on. Lovely as it is."

"Not at all. I like seeing you in my shirt. It's kind of sexy, actually." He grinned wickedly as he walked toward her.

"Oh no you don't, mister!" She threw a hand up. "I need a break!"

He stopped in front of her. "I was just going to kiss you." And with that, he bent down and brushed his lips against hers.

"Oh."

"Yes, well, not that I wouldn't ravish you again if you'd let me." He winked at her, then walked past her to set the glasses and wine down on the dresser. He opened the top drawer and pulled out a pair of boxers, slipping them on. Pouring them each a glass of wine, he handed her one and then sat back on the bed.

"Okay, next question."

"Ugh! Really?" she moaned, hoping he had moved on from this subject.

"I'm just getting started. I'll take whatever pieces of you that you're willing to share, even if it has to be like this."

"Okay, okay." She sat on the bed across from him, pulling her legs into a cross-legged position. "When did you lose your virginity?"

He cocked his head. "Oh, going for the good stuff now, eh? You know you have to answer the same question, right?"

"Yeah, yeah. It's okay, it's not very exciting. It was very standard. I was seventeen, and it was to my high school boyfriend after senior prom."

"Oh, that's romantic, not standard." Drew smiled, examining her a little wistfully, as if imagining a younger version of herself. "Okay, I'm afraid mine probably won't surprise you. Or maybe it will. I was seventeen too, and it was with my sister's nanny, Lisa."

"Oh, you have a sister? Where was she tonight?" Hannah was more surprised at the revelation of a sister then at how he'd lost his virginity.

"Yes. Well, no. Not anymore." Drew's eyes filled with sadness. "I had a sister. Ben and I. A younger sister. Her name was Elizabeth. We called her Lizzie. She died when she was sixteen."

Hannah's hand flew to her mouth as she gasped in surprise. "Drew, I'm so sorry. I wouldn't have asked if I had known."

He shrugged. "How could you have known? It was a long time ago now. Almost fifteen years." He stopped and shook his head. "Wow, when I say it out loud, it's hard to believe how long ago it was."

"Is it okay—I mean; can I ask how? If it's not too hard for you to talk about it?" she asked somberly.

"She was coming home from a dance with some of her friends and their car was hit by a drunk driver. My sister was in the front passenger seat. She and her friend, Mindy, who was driving, were both killed. There were two more girls in the back of the car that ended up okay. Of course, the fucking drunk that hit them didn't have a scratch on him." He shook his head in disgust.

She got up, took his wineglass from his hand, and placed it down with hers as well. She climbed back up on the bed and, not knowing what else to do but needing to do something, took him in her arms and held him. She hugged him hard, wanting him to feel something other than the pain of the memory he'd just shared.

"I'm so sorry. I have a brother and a sister and I can't imagine how I would feel if I lost either of them."

He kissed the top of her head, holding her back before whispering, "Thank you."

Instead of pulling apart, they both lay down on the bed, her back to his front, his arms wrapped around her, holding her close.

"So, you want to ask me anymore of these fun questions?" Drew joked weakly.

"I think I'm afraid to. God knows what kind of stone I'll kick over next if I do!"

"I'm tough. Go ahead and fire away. Besides, it's my only means of learning more about you."

"Always an ulterior motive with you." She laughed. "I was actually just wondering if we had to go back to the estate. Will it be noticed if we don't return soon?"

Behind her, Drew shrugged. "I suppose they'll notice eventually. Do you want to go back?"

She sighed deeply, responding wistfully, "I wish I could stay here forever."

His entire body tightened at her confession. "Then stay."

She laughed nervously, not sure where he was going with this.

"Yes, I'll just stay here in your little castle and you can take care of me forever."

He released her and sat up. She sat up as well and turned toward him, looking him in the eye.

"Well, maybe not forever, but for right now, I'd like you to stay."

"Drew, what are talking about?" Her heart raced.

He stroked her face lovingly. "Scarlett, do you think I've ever brought a sub out of the compound, let alone to my house?" He looked down, shaking his head before continuing. "I don't know what it is. You make me feel something I haven't felt in a long time. Right now, the thought of saying good-bye to you in a few hours already feels wrong. So I'm asking you to stay. I'd like more."

She looked at him, wide-eyed, surprised at his revelation even though she'd suspected he was feeling just as much, if not more, than she was. "Drew, I . . ." She wrung her hands nervously, staring at the diamonds on her wrist.

"I'm scaring you," he stated and then laughed. "I'm scaring myself! I don't say shit like this to anyone."

"It's just that, this isn't my life. Do you understand that? This isn't me. You don't know me. Not really. I'm just being who you want me to be."

"I don't believe that. You can't tell me that what we just shared wasn't you."

"That was just sex." She knew she was lying as she said the words, but she said them anyway. No matter what she might be starting to feel for Drew, she had to consider what—*who* was waiting for her back in the real world, and that was more important than anything she might want.

He scoffed. "That wasn't just sex. And I'm not just talking about the sex. There was a lot more going on there than just sex and you're lying to yourself if you try to pretend otherwise."

"It doesn't matter. This is all I have to give."

He looked at her angrily. "What do you mean it doesn't matter? It doesn't matter that what we have might be something more? Something worth exploring?"

Sadness filled her eyes. "This isn't my life. My life is . . . Well, my life is complicated. And this"—she gestured between them— "this is just a means to an end for me."

Drew's eyes were blazing now. "So, it's back to the money again? Is that all this is to you? A job? The money?"

She flinched. Tears began to form and fall from the corners of her eyes. "I'm sorry. I am, really. Of course this weekend has been amazing. You've been amazing. So much more than I thought it could be. But yes, this is my job. And yes, I need the money." She wiped the tears off her cheeks before continuing. "This is just the way it has to be for me."

Drew stood abruptly, watching as tears slid down Scarlett's cheeks, but unable to contain his anger. "Dammit, it doesn't have to be this way! I'll give you whatever fucking money you need. *Just choose me.*"

He watched in disbelief as she just shook her head slowly, tears streaming down her cheeks now. "I can't. There are reasons that are much bigger than me. I just can't. I'm sorry."

He loomed above her, fury, hurt and confusion ripping through him and then resignation as he spoke. "No. You won't. Because you choose not to. You could. If you wanted to."

He stormed across the room and grabbed his glass of wine on

the dresser, draining it in one long gulp before throwing it across the room, smashing it into a hundred pieces against the wall. Scarlett yelped in surprise, then curled into a ball on the bed.

With long, hard strides, he returned to the bed, grabbing her roughly by the hair and yanking her face up to his. "Then if this is just about the money, I might as well get what I paid for. Get up off this bed. Now!"

Hannah looked at him, eyes wide in fear and disbelief. Her one moment of hesitation had Drew pulling her off the bed by her hair, so she pushed herself up and off the bed before he pulled it clean off her head. When she was standing, he grabbed the neckline of her shirt and ripped it off her in two pieces.

Her body lunged forward with the motion, causing her to cry out in pain as she crashed into him. He snatched her shoulders and, shoving her down onto the bed, held her there with one strong arm.

"Drew, what are you doing? Please stop," she urged, desperation in her voice.

"You don't get to tell me to stop, Scarlett," he hissed in her ear as he bent down to remove his boxers. "I paid for you. I'll do whatever the fuck I want to you. Understood?"

Hannah lay speechless, bewildered, tears running down her face. How had they gotten to this moment so quickly? Drew loomed over her in anger, his actions about to lead him to a place she knew they wouldn't be able to come back from. She did the only thing she could think of to save herself, to save him.

"Ghost. Ghost. Ghost . . ."

It was barely a whisper, but from the look of shock that erupted across his face, it had the impact of a scream. He froze, then jumped back as if someone had dumped a bucket of cold water on him, raising a hand to cover his mouth. *"Fuck."*

She curled up into a sitting position as he looked at her, wide-eyed, his face contorted as if in pain. He took a step toward her again, reaching out, but she flinched back. He stopped, staggering as if he'd been struck.

"Scarlett . . ." He scrubbed a hand through his hair, his eyes blinking rapidly. "I'm sorry. I'm so sorry. Please, forgive me."

Before she could respond, he turned and fled the room, bounding down the stairs. She broke out in sobs as a door slammed below, then pulled a blanket from the bed up and around her body.

When Drew didn't return after a half hour, Hannah got up off the bed and went into the bathroom. She looked at her reflection in the mirror; her face was red and puffy from crying and the outline of the bite mark on her shoulder stood out angrily. She pulled out the pins holding her hair up, letting it fall around her shoulders. She turned the shower on as hot as it would go and stepped in, letting the water run over her.

She scrubbed every inch of her skin, trying to wash away the confusion flowing through her. When she stepped out of the shower, she was surprised to see a clean T-shirt and a pair of sweats sitting on the counter. Drew must have come in while she was showering.

She dried herself off quickly, the towel catching on the diamond choker around her neck. She worked to loosen the snag, and then placing the towel down, she removed the necklace and the bracelet, freeing herself of Drew's invisible hold. She walked into the bedroom and placed them both on the dresser.

After pulling on the sweats and T-shirt and running a brush

through her hair, she tentatively made her way downstairs to find Drew. Her heart was hammering in her chest. Would she find the gentle man who'd worshipped her body earlier, or the monster she'd unleashed with her refusals? Walking into the kitchen, she was startled to find a stranger sitting at the counter, reading a newspaper.

"E-excuse me?" Hannah stammered. "Who are you?"

The man stood up immediately, closing the paper as he did. He was tall and lean, probably in his forties, with close-cropped hair. He was dressed casually in dark jeans and a light grey, button-down shirt. He nodded at her. "Scarlett, I presume?"

"Yes."

"I'm James." He walked up to her while extending his hand in greeting. "Mr. Sapphire asked that I return you to the estate."

She shook his hand absently, confusion still settled on her face. "I'm sorry. Is Drew—I mean, Mr. Sapphire here? I need to speak to him."

James shook his head. "I'm sorry, miss. He's gone."

"Gone?" she repeated.

"Yes, miss." James shifted his feet uncomfortably, clearing his throat before continuing. "Do you have anything you need before we leave?"

She thought about the dress and the shoes. She definitely didn't want or need those again. She saw the clutch still sitting on the counter and, grabbing it, said, "No, let's go."

Her heart felt like lead in her chest. She couldn't believe he'd just left. Without a single word to her. How had this happened? She'd done nothing wrong. She was his submissive. She'd acted as such. But had she? Should she have allowed herself to be taken out of the comfort and the protection that the estate provided her? In doing so, had she allowed Drew to believe that their relationship was something other than what it was meant to be? What was she supposed to do now? So many questions she had no answers for.

She rode to the estate in silence, questions and thoughts spinning in her head. She prayed that Drew's car would be in the driveway when they arrived. Perhaps he'd just needed some time. As they pulled through the gates, the sun was just beginning to rise and lighten the sky, the exact opposite of her own inner horizon.

Pulling into the driveway, her heart sank as she realized Drew's car wasn't there. One of the estate carts was parked along the walkway, though. Who could be here at this hour? James got out of the car, coming around to open the door for her.

"Thank you, James," she said quietly and made her way to the bungalow's front door. As she was reaching for the handle, the door swung open wide, Domme Maria standing in the entryway.

Hannah couldn't disguise her surprise and let out a little gasp. "Oh! Domme Maria, I wasn't expecting you."

"Come in, Scarlett." Domme Maria raised a sleek eyebrow. "I thought you and Drew had gone to a ball? Please tell me that isn't what you wore."

Hannah looked down at Drew's T-shirt and sweats, then shrugged. She wasn't sure what Domme Maria did or didn't know, so she answered vaguely, "My dress got dirty, so Master Drew gave me this to change into."

"Well, I'm sorry he had to cut your time short. I'm sure you'll be happy to know it will have no effect on the fee owed to you." Domme Maria started walking further into the house and beckoned for Hannah to follow. "Come."

Hannah followed her into the kitchen, questions reeling

through her mind. She'd safe-worded. She shouldn't get her whole fee. What had Drew told Domme Maria? "Did you speak to him?"

"Master Drew? No, my assistant did. He explained that he was called away on a business emergency and had to cut your time short but wanted to make sure I saw to your needs personally. Apparently he felt bad. Who knew?"

"Oh, okay." She wasn't sure what to say. Obviously Drew hadn't told Domme Maria what had actually occurred between the two of them, and she definitely wasn't going to expose the truth.

The Domme looked at her skeptically. "Are you all right, Scarlett?"

"Yes, Ma'am. Just tired." She yawned to support her claim.

"Okay, if you say so. My gut is telling me it's something else though. You can talk to me if you need to." Domme Maria clicked her fingernails on the counter as if offering Hannah a chance to speak. After a moment of silence though, she continued. "I've brought your clothes here for you to change into. Once you're done, we can go to the office and I'll provide your weekend payment. Then you'll be free to leave."

"Yes, Ma'am," Hannah said quietly and started to walk toward the bedroom.

"Scarlett," Domme Maria called, "you did amazing for your first auction. Master Drew paid fifty thousand dollars for you, which means you made twelve thousand five hundred dollars."

Hannah stopped in her tracks and turned, staring at the other woman in shock. "What?"

Domme Maria huffed in disbelief. "Oh you silly girl! You have no idea of your worth, do you?"

Hannah shook her head and walked quietly to the bedroom to

change. Domme Maria had no idea just how close to home those words hit.

Chapter Eleven

Two Weeks Later

"Hannah, there's a messenger here for you!" her assistant called from the front of the shop.

"Can you just sign for it, please? I need to finish this arrangement for the Hoovers."

Robin appeared in the doorway of their workspace. "I tried. She says it has to be delivered in person."

Hannah sighed, exasperated, and wiped her hands on her apron as she made her way to the front of the shop. Surprise hit her when she saw that the messenger was none other than her attendant from Baton Timide. Rose looked ethereal as always, dressed in a soft, pink dress that flowed over her willowy body. "Rose? What are you doing here?"

The other woman smiled. "Hello, miss. Maria sent me to deliver this to you." She held out a flat, gift-wrapped package with a card attached. "Given the nature of the gift, she thought it best be delivered in person."

Hannah took the gift, curious. Setting it down on the counter, she opened the enevelope first. The card within was a heavy, cream-colored stock with the initials "AMS" embossed in sapphire blue on the front. Her heart immediately started pounding as she opened the card. Inside was a check for one hundred thousand dollars, a business card for Andrew Matthew Sapphire and a message written in what had to be Drew's handwriting.

Scarlett,

Please take this and use it for whatever drove you to Baton Timide. I know you quit, and I know I drove you to it. What's in the box belongs to you. I can't imagine it on another. I am sorrier than any words could ever express. I miss you. Please call me.

Drew

Hannah's hands shook as she set the card and its contents down on the counter and broke the seal on the wrapping covering the box. She knew in her heart what it was, but as she tore a corner of the paper and saw Tiffany blue beneath, her breathing stopped. It was the diamond choker necklace she had worn to the ball. Her collar. She looked up at Rose in shock.

"Rose, I can't take this." She pushed the box across the counter, then lifted the check and placed it on top of the box as well. "Please, please, just take these back."

Rose placed her hand over Hannah's, squeezing it in understanding. "Of course, miss. Whatever you wish."

Rose gathered the box and check and placed them in the bag on her shoulder. Before leaving, she asked Hannah one final question. "Do you have a message for Mr. Sapphire?"

Hannah shook her head as a single tear fell down her cheek,

which she quickly wiped away.

"Is he— I mean— Have you seen him?"

Rose kindly shook her head. "I'm sorry, miss. I haven't."

Rose gave Hannah one last kindhearted look and left the shop, the bell over the door tinkling as she did. Hannah took the note and business card and walked back into the workshop, where Robin was finishing an arrangement.

"What was all that about?" Robin asked.

Hannah shook her head. "Oh, nothing. A misunderstanding. I took care of it." The bell to the door sounded again, notifying them of another customer. "Why don't you go take care of that? I'll just put the finishing touches on this."

"You got it." Robin bounced out of the room.

Hannah walked across the room and placed the note and card under the silk mask that lay discreetly on the shelf above her desk. After Drew had walked away from her two weeks ago, she'd quit Baton Timide, realizing she wasn't the kind of person who could turn her heart off, as much as she had hoped she could be. She'd deposited the money she had been paid into a savings account, not wanting to see or think about it again. She had done the same with her emotions and feelings for Drew, locking them away deep inside her, and buried herself in her work instead.

Two Days Later

"What do you mean she sent it back?" Drew slammed his fist down on Domme Maria's desk.

"Andrew, you need to calm down, please." Maria spoke coolly. "She doesn't want it. I can't force her to take it."

"Did you include the note I gave you?" His voice was lower, more even this time.

"I did, even though it was against my better judgment."

He ran a hand through his hair, frustration his reigning emotion, and sighed.

"You understand that this is completely inappropriate? A submissive's identity is to remain private unless *she* allows it to be otherwise."

He brought his gaze up to meet Maria's, fire blazing between them. "You think I don't know that? You think I want to feel this way? Act this way?"

"You're a Master Dominant. This is a situation you should have never allowed yourself to be in. I'm not going to lie here. I'm extremely disappointed in your behavior. Plus, I've lost a beautiful submissive."

He scoffed. "That makes two of us." A look of pleading entered his eyes. "Please, I'm begging. Tell me her name or where I can find her."

"I'd never thought I would see the day you begged me for something, but you need to let her go. She's made her decision and you have to respect that." Maria spoke firmly, but a note of compassion snuck through.

Drew dropped his head into his hands, nodding in defeat. "I know, Maria. I know."

Two Months Later

Drew and Ben made their way out of the restaurant and across the large marble lobby of the hotel. They had just finished lunch and had decided to play hooky for the rest of the afternoon after they grabbed Drew's car from the valet. Ben's cane clicked on the marble floor as they walked but was overshadowed by the laughter they shared.

Ben pointed to the reception desk. "Hey, isn't that your friend Scarlett?"

Drew skidded to a halt as his gaze darted to the desk. Scarlett. She was holding an ex-travagant arrangement of roses and talking to the concierge animatedly. Her long hair was up in a ponytail, and she was dressed in jeans and a T-shirt. She looked just like an ordinary girl.

"I guess hitting the track is out?" Ben grumbled.

Drew pulled his gaze away from Scarlett long enough to respond, "Yeah, sorry, Benny," and then he hurried across the room. When he reached her, he touched her shoulder to get her attention. "Scarlett?"

She spun around quickly, surprise splashed across her face, the large arrangement of roses slipping from her hands, crashing to the ground, glass shattering, water spilling in a pool at their feet.

"Jesus, Scarlett!" Drew pulled her back safely away from the broken glass. "Are you okay? I'm sorry, I didn't mean to startle you."

She didn't say a thing. Just stood there, staring at him like he might not be real.

Drew barked at the desk clerk, "You there! Can you please get someone to take care of this?"

The clerk picked up the phone, dialing a number while saying, "Yes, sir, Mr. Sapphire."

All of a sudden, a thousand pieces clicked into place for Hannah, and she laughed a little desperately. "Oh my god! Of course, Andrew Sapphire. Sapphire Luxury Resorts."

Drew dismissed her revelation with a quick head shake and took her elbow, leading her away from the front desk and the mess they had created. Once again, he asked, "Scarlett, are you okay?"

She finally looked at him, shaking her head in disbelief, and repeated, "Oh my god. You're Andrew fucking Sapphire. You *own* Sapphire Resorts? How did I not put the pieces together before?"

"Stop saying that. My family owns it. Not just me. It's not that big of a deal," Drew replied.

"Not that big of a deal? Are you kidding me? You're a gazillionaire!"

"So maybe you should have kept the gifts I sent you then Scarlett. Obviously I can afford it." His voice was gruff.

"Stop calling me Scarlett," she retorted.

He glared right back at her and gritted out, "I'll call you anything you want me to, but since I don't know your real name, it puts me at a bit of a disadvantage."

The concierge walked over to them then, pointing to the flowers strewn across the lobby floor. "Excuse me, Hannah dear, what would you like me to tell Mr. Ruffino about the flowers for his wife?"

She looked at Drew, quickly realizing that now he at least knew her first name, before responding to the concierge. "George, would you be so kind as to call him and explain what happened? I'll pop back to the shop, put together a new arrangement and have it here within an hour."

"Of course. Thank you!"

Drew looked at her like he was seeing her for the first time and then took a step toward her. He swept a stray lock of hair from her face, back behind her ear, then cupped her cheek. "Hannah. It suits you."

For one moment, she forgot where she was and leaned into his touch, but then she took a step back. "Drew, Andrew, Mr. Sapphire, whatever I should call you. I'm sorry. I have to go."

She turned and started walking toward the exit. Drew grabbed her arm, stopping her. "Scar-- Hannah, wait! You're just going to leave?"

She turned back, her feet weighed down with grief. "Drew, I have to go. I have a job to do. I'm sorry, but nothing has changed for me."

"Please. Five minutes. Let's talk. Let's figure this out. I've missed you."

The pain and desperation in Drew's eyes broke her heart. Seeing him again caused every emotion she had finally managed to lock down over the last month to come screaming back to the surface. She so badly wanted to stay, to listen to what he had to say, to feel what she felt when she was in his arms again. But instead, she kissed him softly on the cheek. "Good-bye, Drew." And then she walked away, leaving him there staring after her.

As soon as Hannah was through the doors, her hand flew to her mouth to hold in the sobs trying to escape. She ran to the delivery van she'd left in short-term parking and hopped in quickly, shutting the door on all the emotions she was feeling for Drew.

Drew stood frozen in the lobby for a good three minutes before he made the decision to go after her. He could wait for her to return with the flower delivery, but he was betting that she would send someone else with it. He walked back in the direction of the concierge and, scaring him half to death, called out, "George!"

The concierge pointed to himself in question. "Me, sir?"

"Yes, you!" Exasperated. "Tell me what you know about Hannah!"

"Hannah with the flowers?" he asked.

"Yes, yes! Hannah with the flowers. What do you know?" Drew wanted answers and he wanted them quickly.

"N-nothing, really," he stammered. "I only know she works at The Secret Garden Boutique. That's it. She prepares special arrangements for some of our guests from time to time."

"Good, that's good. Okay, thank you." Drew clapped him on the shoulder before walking away. He gave the valet his ticket and, as he was waiting, googled the address to The Secret Garden. This time she was going to talk to him and he wasn't going to take no for an answer.

Fifteen minutes later, Drew was driving past her shop. It was in a particularly busy part of town, so he had to park a few buildings down and across the street. After finally finding a spot, he got out and was about to cross the street when he saw Hannah walk out of the shop, a smile spread wide across her face.

His eyes looked in the direction hers were focused and then opened wide. A little girl was skipping down the sidewalk, holding the hand of a man wearing camo fatigues. Drew could see that the little girl was the spitting image of Hannah, the same blonde hair, the same brown eyes. When the little girl spotted Hannah, she released the man's hand and began running toward her, shouting, "Mommy! Mommy!"

Hannah bent down, caught her daughter in her arms and brought her up in a hug, kissing her on top of her little head. The man had reached them now too and bent down, placing a kiss on Hannah's cheek in greeting.

Drew watched the scene unfold before his eyes, his breath caught in his throat, his heart thumping wildly. *She's married? She has a child?*

Hannah swung the young girl up on her hip and, as she turned to walk back into the shop, caught movement out of the corner of her eye. Looking up, she saw Drew standing across the street, eyes locked on her in apparent shock. She met his gaze for one quick second and shook her head, silently mouthing, "No!" and then turned and walked into the shop with her family.

Coming Soon

Michelle Windsor's second book, and the conclusion to The Auction Series, The Final Bid, will be out in April 2017. Here's a sneak peek.

The Final Bid, Book Two of The Auction Series

Drew leaned against the brick wall of the alley, each heavy breath leaving him in a puffy white cloud. It was early November and mornings were dawning chillier each day. He pulled the hood of his sweatshirt tighter over his head and then stuffed his hands into the front pocket to try and insulate some of the warmth his body had created during his run. He'd arrived earlier than the previous mornings, and had been waiting in the alley across from the flower shop for almost a half hour.

It had been four days since he'd ran into her in the lobby of his hotel. Four days since he discovered she had a child and a husband. Four days of gut twisting agony. He knew he shouldn't be here, but each morning here he was; hidden in the shadows like a thief, waiting to steal another look at her. Scarlett. *Hannah.* There were so many questions he wanted to ask her, but she made it crystal clear she didn't want to see him again when she looked straight at him and said 'No'. So, here he was, waiting and watching. Trying to figure out what to do next, but needing to see her in the meantime. Even if it was just a stolen glance.

His heart started beating violently in his chest and he pushed himself back further into the shadows as he saw the door on the side of the alley open. He watched as Hannah stepped out through the doorway, and then a second, smaller image of her shuffle out behind and wait while her mother locked the door. His eyes remained fixed on them as he observed Hannah take her daughter's hand and guide her out of the alley before buckling her into the delivery van and driving away.

Like the previous mornings, twenty minutes later, the now familiar van pulled back into the alley beside the shop. The brake lights burned a bright red before turning dark as the sound of the engine died. He heard the van door open, close and then a moment later saw her emerge between the wall and the van. Today she wore a black wool coat and had a bright pink scarf wrapped around her neck, her nose buried in it's warmth as she walked quickly to the front door of the flower shop. Her hair, the color of gold, was a stark contrast to the coat as it flowed loose and wavy down over her back. He knew that if he could get close enough and lean into her, she would smell like flowers.

Drew continued to watch as she unlocked the metal casing covering the door, then slid it up and out of the way. The metal must be cold because she was rubbing her hands together while blowing her breath on them. She found another key on the set she held and unlocked the interior door of the shop, opening it and walking in, closing it behind her, the faint tinkling of the bell carrying on the breeze. He stayed for another thirty minutes, waiting to see if this morning would be any different than the last three. It wasn't. Her co-worker arrived just before 8:00 a.m. and a delivery truck full of flowers a few minutes later. He popped his earbuds back in, pushed play on his iPod, and with his head down began the run back to the hotel before she came out to meet the delivery driver.

Acknowledgements

This may be the hardest part of the book to write for me because there are so many people that helped and encouraged me along the way, not only in writing this book, but in making me believe I could actually do this. I apologize in advance for my wordiness-my editor will be shaking her head I'm sure...

To the person who has been there for me since the very beginning, I must first and foremost thank my mom, Sandy Erickson. She's ALWAYS been my number one fan. From the time I started writing in high school, she would read my work and always, always encourage me to keep going and tell me she couldn't wait to see what was going to happen next. Well Mom, it took me awhile, but I finally finished one for you. I promise I'll keep my fingers working overtime for you.

To my boys; all three of you. Doug, Tyler and Tommy; you who make my world go round and complete it with your love and laughter. Doug, thank you the very most for pushing me to follow my dreams, and for giving me the space to do it. For making dinner for the boys when I lost track of time and didn't realize it was way past a reasonable time to feed them. Who knew boys needed to eat so much?? For helping with the laundry, their homework, our crazy houseful of animals, but mostly, just for loving me the way that you do. No one, and I mean no one, could ever make me feel as special as you, and even though I'm positive I don't say it enough, I love you so much. Tyler, thanks for understanding when I asked you not to play your drums or hook your guitar up to your amp, and still being able to make the most beautiful music. I heart you so much. Tommy, for always asking how my book is going, how many likes I have on my page, and for making sure I always had a drink or a snack; my cup runneth over at the love I have for you.

To my sisters, Tammy, Laura and Karla; thanks for always having my back and for loving me no matter what. I know I'm the bossy one, and the jealous one, and the emotional one... but you know I love you so hard and couldn't imagine a world without you three. Seriously, you girls are my best, best friends and the loves of my life. After wine, tequila and my books of course... ;)

To my friends, Robin, Julie, and Joel. Thank you for so much for all the support and words of encouragement you've given me over the last six months. You literally lifted me up some days with your words of praise and belief in me. Joel, you should get a special award for listening to me talk so much about this book and how much it meant for me to be writing it. You asked me endless questions, I'm sure to appease my self-doubts, (as well as keeping Doug from talking any more smack about the Cowboys), but your constant interest and your intelligence really did drive me to work harder at creating the best work I could. Robin and Julie, the two of you are without a doubt the best support system a girl could have. From bringing me Prosecco to celebrate milestones, to endless 'how are you doing and can I do anything for you' texts, for talking me off the cliffs I came so precariously close to jumping off of on more than one occasion, you are always there when I need you. You're the best of the best. I love you girls, so, so much. Sinseriously.

Finally, I want to thank three authors that had a profound impact on my life over the last two years, and ultimately led me to begin writing again. First is Erica Stevens. Two years ago, I bought one of her books, (Captured), and devoured it in one sitting. I picked up the next book in the series, and shortly thereafter, the next one. I fell in love with her writing and her story and wanted so badly to tell her. So, I did something I had never done before; I found her on Facebook and sent a message telling her exactly how I felt. And – OH MY GOD! – She actually wrote back to me. That had never happened to me before. A real live author was talking to me about her book. She asked me to be on her street team, which I of course accepted, and from there was introduced to another world I had no idea existed; The Indie World. (Yes, I put it in caps. It's another dimension as far as I'm concerned.) Introduction to this new world was like an awakening for me. I discovered authors, made some amazing friends, (Gina, Connie, Gretchen, Amanda, Rory, Donna), started my own blog, and learned how possible it was for a person to publish their own work if they wanted to. Along the way, I stumbled across Casey Clipper, and after reading all her books, started bothering her (ok, I think we became friends, even though she likes the Steelers), and learned even more about the author community. Casey, thank you so much for answering my endless questions about publishing my book. You were so helpful and always willing to help, never once losing your patience or blocking me (hee hee). I aspire to one day be able to help guide a new author the way you've so generously helped me. You are a diamond in this sometimes rough neighborhood and your friendship is treasured. The last author, whom I sure has no idea that I exist, (even though one may classify me as a stalker if my search/view history was checked), is Colleen Hoover. She's a big name in this industry, and for those of you who know her, and her work, will hopefully agree that her writing is a step above brilliant and the humanitarian work (I think this is what it should be referred as), she does define a new level of generosity that we should all aspire to. See, I told you I love her. Probably too much. But in all seriousness, it's not her books, or the work she does to give back to others, it's her personal story that inspired me. She's just a normal girl, (I mean, there are some that might question this), married, with three boys, trying to get through life like the rest of us. Some days harder than others, barely struggling to get by. She gets brave, she gets bold and decides to start writing again, even though she knows, from earlier attempts, that she probably isn't going to make a living from this, but she does it anyway, just cause she loves to write.   And you know what, two years later, she's written numerous best selling books, is published internationally, supports her entire family, (and others I'm sure), and has a fan base that adores her. She was the little train that could. She was the Horton who heard a Who and actually listened. She was... ok, you get the point. And the point is, is that she just went for it. And she did it. She did what so many of us dream of doing. So, I thought, I can do this. And so I did it...

About the Author

Michelle Windsor is a full-time working mom of two teenage boys, one grown daughter, and wife to one seriously amazing husband. She lives in a suburb about 25 miles north of Boston, Massachusetts with her two dogs, two cats and two birds. She jokes that all she needs is an Ark and she could set sail.

Her love of reading started with Laura Ingalls Wilder and The Little House on The Prairie Series, and fell in love with writing as a teenager. She always dreamed of writing, and may have even started a few stories over the years, and finally got the nerve up to share some of her wicked imagination with you.

You can find her at any of the social media sites below, as well as on Amazon and Goodreads. Please stop by and say hello. She loves to make new friends, aka stalkers. Sign-up for her newsletter to stay up to date with any new releases and events.

And of course, she would love it if you left a review of your thoughts on this book on Amazon. It can be two sentences or a whole series of thoughts. Every review left helps to get an author recognized.

Made in the USA
Columbia, SC
17 September 2021